show your love
and support!
Much love! ♡
Michelle xo

# BLACK DANDY

## FICTION FOR THE FEARLESS

Black Dandy is a quarterly literary journal
dedicated to excellence in magic realism,
surrealism, and the otherwise strange.

Based in New Zealand, we're proud to
feature top talent from around the world.

www.blackdandy.co

EDITOR & DESIGNER: H. Andrew Lynch CO-EDITOR: Audrey Lynch
ARTIST: Lance Jackson
CONTRIBUTORS: Soramimi Hanarejima, Addy Evenson, Thomas Kearnes,
James Rowland, Jay Caselberg, Jennifer Benningfield, Tom Weller,
Chris Kuriata, Michelle Willms, Matthew Lyons
**BLACK DANDY, ISSUE 2**
www.blackdandy.co

# CONTENTS

# BLACK DANDY

# WHEN TO USE WHAT HAS BEEN SAVED

## SORAMIMI HANAREJIMA

Your swift, sweeping strides through the house close what little is left of the gap between your singular, urgent intention to enter the Extra Time Room and the room itself. But as you cross the kitchen, mere steps from your desperately desired destination, your pace slows as a smile softens your face and then your mood. Here's where it all began.

You had just finished your homework—one of those fill-in-the-blank worksheets you'd get daily during second grade. The rest of the evening now lay before you, free of schoolwork, and you were eager to crack open your newly checked-out library book. That's when your father called you and Tamporé to the kitchen for a family meeting. You were sure the topic of discussion would be, once again, chores.

Feeling the meeting to itself be a chore, you lumbered into the kitchen to find both your parents were already there, waiting. But the chairs around the kitchen table were not waiting; they had not been pulled out as they always were before these meetings, ready for the members of your family to take their places. Your mother and father were just standing by the counter, so you followed their example and simply stood by the refrigerator. A few seconds later, your little sister came in, and seeing everyone standing, she stood next to you.

"Look at the clock above the sink," your mother said, presumably starting this family meeting. "What's time does it read?"

"Seven twenty four," Tamporé answered proudly. She had recently learned how to read analog clocks.

"Right, Tam," your mother said. "Now, all of us are going into the room that used to be the study, and we'll play a game there."

"Oh, *oh*, how about Race to Rainbows?" Tamporé blurted.

"Sure," your father answered. "I'll go

get it from the game shelf and meet you outside the room."

Once everyone was gathered by the door he had painted a creamy sea-foam green just days before, your father turned to your mother and said, "How about you do the honors?"

So with a fluid twist of her wrist and extension of her arm, she opened the door that had been closed for weeks. Then your mother swept an open hand across the threshold to invite you and your sister to enter.

After stepping into the room for the first time since the redecorating began, you took a moment to savor the fresh coziness of the new custard-yellow wallpaper and pastel-plaid throw rugs, all warmly lit with portable lanterns. Then your family of four sat around the small coffee table in the middle of the room, upon which your father began dealing out the cards of Tamporé's favorite game.

Soon, the game and the room's atmosphere melded into a homey ambiance. Aside from the newness of the decor and novelty of lantern lighting, the room was similar to the other rooms in the house; compact but not cramped, furnished just enough to feel lived-in and inviting—a space laughter could easily fill and enliven. In retrospect, you should have noticed one thing that made this room different: the windows were unusually dark, even for a November evening. But you were too caught up in the game to make this observation. The room and your mind were full of excitement that was rare for a school night—the delight of devising promising strategies combined with the thrilling uncertainty of what cards

would be played as you waited your turn. You still remember that your sister won the first two rounds, your mother the last; you came very close to being the victor of the second round with three golden sunrises.

After the fourth round, your father said in his gentle and jovial way, "All right that's enough for tonight."

Your family returned to the kitchen, where your mother asked you and Tamporé, "What time does the kitchen clock read now?"

You had to be reading it wrong.

That was your first reaction. It had to be 8:26. There was no way it could be only 7:26. But no matter how you tilted your head or squinted your eyes, the clock's short, red hand lay between the 7 and 8.

Just how was that possible?

Your father smiled when you looked to him in confusion, then said, "That clock is working just fine. That's the correct time, out here."

"Check the clock in your room," your mother encouraged, also smiling.

You and Tamporé scampered upstairs. On the night stand between your bed and hers, the clock's lines of magenta light read 7:27.

*Are Mom and Dad playing a trick on us?* you wondered.

Eager to know why these two clocks did not agree with your sense of time, you and your sister hurried back into the kitchen.

Your mother's blue eyes seemed especially bright as she gave you the explanation that your young minds, creative as they were, had little hope of figuring out.

"Time in the room passes differently from the time outside it. While we were playing Race to Rainbows inside, time was passing *very* slowly out here," she told you.

She pointed down the hallway, then continued.

"In that room, we use *extra time*. Time that we have in addition to time that's normally passing. In there, that's where we're going to keep time we don't need right away. Dad and I will collect bits of extra time and chunks of time that are uncommitted. We'll put everything we can collect in there."

"What does *un-com-mitted* mean?" Tamporé asked, as if trying not to drop this word when verbally handling it for the first time.

"Uncommitted time is time you don't have plans to use. Committed time is time that we've promised to someone or something. Time that we've made plans to use," your father explained. "Like you have to be in school tomorrow from nine in the morning to three in the afternoon. That part of your day is committed. That's committed time."

"It's time that we can't just do whatever we want with," you added.

Your sister nodded thoughtfully.

"Right," your mother said, pleased by your contribution. "So if I have five extra minutes when I get home, before we have to get dinner ready, I'll put those uncommitted minutes in that room. And by saving uncommitted time in there, someday when we really *really* need more time, we'll have the time we need, in that room—our Extra Time Room."

You understood your mother's explanation but could not relate to it, could not yet appreciate the significance.

To you and Tamporé, time seemed abundant enough. The only occasions when time ran out too quickly were during recess and holiday trips. Your tenuous grasp of your mother's words was enabled solely by the adventure movies you liked to watch. Their heroes and heroines were always running out of time, and though they always got through the wormhole before it closed or arrived with the antidote before the poison did any permanent harm, extra time would have been helpful. With it, they could have avoided some of the sacrifices they had to make. But you couldn't imagine your family ending up in those kinds of situations.

So you asked, "When would we really need more time?"

"What would you do if our house were on fire?" your father asked in return.

"Get outside to our meeting point," Tamporé answered quickly while you tried to figure out how a burning home connected to the Extra Time Room.

"Right," your father said. "But what if the smoke were really thick, choking you and stinging your eyes?"

Sensing that there was just one right answer for this, you and Tamporé waited for it.

After a half minute of silence, your father said, "Well, you could run into the Extra Time Room to get some air. While you're inside the room, everything outside would be happening *extremely* slowly, so you could breathe easily for a few minutes without having to worry about the fire getting much bigger. You could even wash the smoke out of your eyes with water from the pitcher we'll keep in there."

You and your sister nodded. The hypothetical situation meshed with the emergency-preparedness lessons you'd both had at school.

"And we're only going to use the Extra Time Room for emergencies like that," your mother said.

The discussion ended on this note, with your mother further stressing that this stash of temporal surplus was to be reserved solely for situations of exceptional need. She made it clear that you were to conduct yourself as if the room wasn't there and would only spring into existence in the most dire moments.

Your mind, however, soon formed a habit of turning your thoughts toward the Extra Time Room whenever you became frantically upset, certain that you were facing circumstances of catastrophic consequence. You would then implore your parents to let you use just a little of the time in there, and they would respond with furrowed brows and harsh words, contending that the situations you felt to be desperate were acutely overblown. Feeling unfairly rebuffed, you'd withdraw and sulk for hours or even days afterward. But as the years passed, you came to retrospectively agree with their judgement, seeing the pattern in hindsight: in your moments of distress, extra time would have been useful but not essential, not deserved.

A couple minutes to check and make sure you had everything in your backpack for the class field trip to the cognitive-archaeology site, before dashing out to catch the bus. Five minutes after breakfast to look over the words for the spelling test you forgot about. Three minutes to dry your eyes and freshen up so Rui-na wouldn't know that you'd been crying when she

came over to pick up library books. Fifteen minutes of private time, to be away from the family reunion after your cousin Limg had "accidentally" thrown a snowball right in your face then called you a wimp because you were upset and demanded an apology.

When you thought back on those episodes in the months and years following them, you couldn't believe you had asked to use the Extra Time Room for such minor, self-centered needs. Of course your had parents denied these requests; how could your childish issues possibly have been worth all the minutes of relaxation and conversation, all the afternoons of outings with friends and contemplative walks that your parents had given up to become precious hours of refuge from future calamities?

Your reflection cultivated a tardy respect for their unyielding restriction on the room's use. And it wasn't long before that respect solidified into complete deference, thanks to your last attempt to use the Extra Time Room.

Your days in fifth grade were drawing to a close, bringing you to the end of your time in elementary school. To conclude this epoch of your education, your final assignment for the school year was to create a story that assembled all the important ideas you had learned since kindergarten. Working diligently weeks ahead of the deadline, you were confident you would finish early. Yet, there you were, alone at the kitchen table the night before the due date, drawing and writing as quickly as you could without making mistakes. But no matter how swiftly your pen moved, each glance at the clock made it despondently clearer that the remaining chapters (which you didn't even have rough drafts of) could not be finished by the approaching deadline.

Suddenly, your vision was blurring with tears that then fell upon and soaked into the blue tablecloth when you blinked them away.

As you wiped the wetness from your eyes, a scenario for the remainder of the night assembled itself your mind. You would enter the Extra Time Room at 11:03pm, work just as hard on your assignment until completion was within your grasp, then exit the Extra Time Room to finish the remaining work and go to bed by about midnight—the hour you had long feared and revered as the intimidating gateway to tomorrow.

This plan felt thick with plausibility, urgency and even inevitability. You were sure this time your parents would agree with you. They talked with such fervor and frequency about the importance of doing well in school and about the necessity of getting enough sleep.

So you rushed into the living room and frantically proposed this plan to your mother and father. In their armchairs, they listened to you make your case and said nothing until you were done. Then, as a part of your mind that had remained quiet already knew would happen, they refused.

"I'm disappointed that you're even asking," your mother said.

Faced with rejection firmer than you had expected, you lost your remaining shreds of composure.

"You have to let me!" you cried, no longer worried about waking your sister with your words.

"You are in no position to tell your father and I what we have to do," your mother said sternly.

"Just a few hours in the room," you pleaded in tears.

"No, darling," your father said, unstirred by your panic. "You cannot use what we've saved there to make up for the time management skills you have not yet mastered. You will not master them this way."

"Only this *once*," you insisted. "Then I'll work harder at planning my schedule."

"We cannot allow you the luxury of using what may later be a necessity," he said, so succinctly, as though he had been planning to tell you that for a long time.

"I thought you were saving it to help us. I need help *right now*," you rebutted, voice becoming shrill.

Your mother looked on at the exchange between you and your father, her face creased hard with irritation.

When you think back to this moment, you are drawn to wonder if your mother wanted to swiftly rise from her armchair and slap you for being so bratty. But this musing of yours is, you suspect, a reflection of how you feel toward your preadolescent self, and not, you hope, a foreshadowing of how you might one day feel toward your own children.

Every second that passed as you stood before your parents brought you closer to sobbing uncontrollably.

Until your father surprised you by saying, "Okay, then I'll help you. I can do some of what you need time to do."

That settled the matter.

Several years later, you would become curious if at this point your father had undermined his attempts to teach you the importance of time management by showing you that people who care about you would be willing to shoulder the responsibilities you had failed to uphold. You would then conclude that he was teaching you another lesson: when you care about someone, you help them do what they don't have time left to do alone, and then sometimes a lack of time can be overcome by generosity and cooperation.

It was still a tiring night of writing and drawing and rewriting and redrawing at the kitchen table, but you didn't go through it alone, and together you and your father finished your story, with enough time left for a few hours of sleep.

A couple weeks later, when you heard about the approaching asteroids, a lurid lucidity sunk into you, as though infusing itself irrevocably into your very being. The completion of a school assignment just couldn't compare to other uses for the room. And you had turned family versus world into parents versus child. The margin of safety your mother and father had grafted to your home, this modicum of protection they had made for you and your sister, it was supposed to provide peace of mind, but you had turned it into a source of stress what seemed like countless times.

During those nerve-racking days of early summer, you could feel it everywhere you went. A veneer of normalcy over sheer dread—people going about their usual routines not knowing how much longer this world (which many now realized they had come to love) would last. This produced in your behavior a veneer of normalcy over sheer shame.

Along with everyone else, your whole family followed the news of the asteroid swarm closely for weeks, until astronomers confirmed that they would all miss the Earth and Moon, narrowly. No one said anything about your outburst during or after what would later be referred to as The Closest Brush. Your mother, father and Tamporé all knew how humbled you felt, and you were grateful that no one rubbed in how self-centered you had been that night just weeks earlier. But sometimes, you wished they had said something, so that there would have been some landmark scolding or snippy remark to put this episode in its place, instead of the silence that let it stretch out and slowly attenuate.

Back then, however, there were barely a few days in the room—an appreciable amount of time but a mere fraction of the current temporal contents of the room. Back then, the demands upon you were not nearly as great as those facing you now. Back then, your needs were more modest, and it was much easier for someone to help you. Back then, you didn't have the responsibility of helping other people, of defending their dreams.

Now, with your hand on the door knob—leathery as if with a patina of memories—you feel even greater certainty that your urgent need to be in the Extra Time Room is legitimate and reasonable. You require only a little of what has been amassed in there—to be the time that your schedule hasn't left you to rest, to reflect, to be with your own thoughts and leave behind those you're paid to have. You will use mere hours out of several months. Hours you can pay back soon, with interest too.

"Look," you'll say to your disapproving mother, showing her your calendar. "I have a vacation coming up that I'm not going to need all of."

The door swings open swiftly, much more easily than you expected, as if you had anticipated pushing against the weight of months on the other side of the door.

*Have the hinges been oiled?*

You can only recall two times when you yourself opened this door, and the last time you were only twelve. Your mother had asked you to move the rocking chair into the Extra Time Room. Minutes later, you were dragging in that worn, wooden antique, which seemed heavier than it needed to be, its weight making it unquestionably part of the adult world you had begun to inhabit and not simply visit. You couldn't imagine anyone sitting in it, upon its hard seat and back like a fence of dowels. You've always thought the sofa here to be exceedingly comfortable and suspected your mother just wanted the rocking chair stored away somewhere.

You step in, switch on the battery-powered lantern hanging to the left of the doorframe, then close the door behind you. Inside, you unhurriedly take in lungfuls of the long-sequestered ambiance of familial warmth, the air animating as you do so, stirring to life with a springtime freshness, from the last time the windows were opened for ventilation.

You sink into the sofa you remember sitting helplessly upon, the cushions sluggishly, almost reluctantly compressing under the pressure of your body as they did that morning your family was going to say goodbye to Aunt Zona, when Tamporé needed time to calm down—time in which her sudden outburst could abate, in which her emotions could run out more of their course. You try not to think about how heavily she was sobbing, how erratically she gasped for air as your mother held her shuddering, closed up form.

Looking around the room, you find packaged water and cases of MREs in the far corner. These supplies puzzle you for a moment. They are in none of your memories of the Extra Time Room, but maybe you never paid attention to them before. The other items here are just as you remember them, in their familiar places. The flashlights, candles, matches, first-aid kit, flare gun and OTC meds are arrayed out on the little table by the inky-black windows facing the backyard. Your father insisted these items be left out so that no time here was expended to get them out if they were needed.

Your gaze lingers upon the physically small but psychologically hefty rules on the far wall.

> *Breathe deeply.*
> *Really listen to each other and yourself.*
> *Give each other the benefit of the doubt.*
> *No arguing.*
> *Start the timer.*

The list looks exactly as it did when your parents hung it up. Typed words on paper sandwiched between sheets of glass locked in place by a brushed steel rectangle. That elegant yet austere frame now reminds you of just how seriously your parents treated this space and makes you aware of the possible purposes they saw the room serving. Seeing these rules also reminds you to run the timer.

*I'll start it in a moment*, you tell yourself.

The softness of the sofa's worn leather conspires with the faint scent of old sweaters and blankets to lull you into a slow mental waltz of gently luminous, nostalgic ideas. The treehouse town. Autumn afternoons on the empty stretch of beige and blue beach. The belief in eternal best friends. Hazy, mythic creatures that coalesce out of vapor. The possibility that life's mysteries could be revealed through art.

Scenes, musings and feelings swirl lightly around your rarefying consciousness with a leisurely but intentional geometry mixed with a graceful spontaneity. They coax you into letting go of what little is left of your patience, letting it rest from its tiring task of holding the irritations of the world at bay, of keeping the the floodgates of your consciousness closed.

Spinning so tranquilly, the dreamy imagery and warm sentiments displace who you were so inevitably a few hours ago, who you had to be in that oppressive conference room as months of your team's work was shredded by a tirade jagged with expletives and sharp, cold facts—to which you said nothing so you could just get it all over with. You could only be a person who abdicated what little agency was left, who did not have the emotional wherewithal to respond to Luminda's pleading eyes, wide with disbelief as the axe came down upon your team's circadian-synchronized, time-sharing basis

for collaborative subconscious cognition— what you still believe to be the best bet for preserving the remaining sanctity of emotional processing in a society where it is under siege. But ever hostile attitudes towards your team's project had made you taciturn, accepting of the fatalism forced upon you.

That outwardly stoic, inwardly exhausted self of yours is now being swept aside by the inseparable siblings of who you have been and who you could be. And now you come to viscerally know the kind of rest you've long needed. Not time to regain some of the stamina depleted by nauseating freak-out-burnout cycles, but time to recover who you are at heart—to be the selves you could not otherwise afford to be.

*Explanations and recourse can be sought later,* they tell you. *For now, remember all that you are.*

When sleep fades away, it recedes to yield the awareness that you're curled up on the sofa in the Extra Time Room. A blanket is—has been draped over you. You open your eyes and find your mother in the rocking chair. Your body jerks quickly into a bolt upright position.

"It must have been only a few hours," you blurt just as automatically as you went from being horizontal to vertical, not yet conscious enough to be more deliberately articulate.

Looking relaxed and contented, your mother smiles lightly and says, "It's time to put to good use the modest wealth we've bestowed upon ourselves."

You stare into her eyes, which are the

calmest you've ever seen them—the brilliant
blue of her irises present nowhere else here
except in your own.

# ALIVE

## ADDY EVENSON

– 1 –

"I saw him again."

Cheryl undid her black buttons. The shirt fell to her ankles.

"We'll get you on some meds," Stephen said.

"I don't like them."

"It's anti-anxiety. It's not speed."

"It makes your brain flat. I need my energy. It helps me create."

"You're dealing with a chemical imbalance. Or! Babe, you know, you should try some mindfulness exercises."

Cheryl took off her skirt.

She fell into the king bed. Into the white blankets. Stephen touched her hand.

She pulled away.

"I just want to go to sleep."

– 2 –

In the morning, Stephen had gone. Cheryl went into the shower. She ran it for a few minutes. The blue lights hummed.

The silence stretched out. Underneath the bathroom counter, beneath the cotton balls, isopropyl alcohol dripped. The floor smelled.

In the next room, Eugenia, the housekeeper, feather dusted the armoire.

"Eugenia," Cheryl said. "Please, be careful under the bathroom sink."

"I didn't touch under the bathroom sink, ma'am."

"Stephen doesn't ever open it, and I know it wasn't me," Cheryl said. "I'm careful."

"But I...yes ma'am. Yes. It won't happen again."

"Good.  Hey, what's the weather?"

"The weather today is having a light breeze."

"Light jacket, pantsuit, black pumps." Cheryl looked at her hair in the mirror. "Blowout," she said.

After Cheryl left, Eugenia took a rag to the bathroom floor.

– 3 –

*Ringgggggggggggggg,
Ringggggggggggggggggg—I'll have my
secretary send one down for you—"Silk
or chiffon,"—If you are asking me this
question, you should not have a job here—
Trish, there are a hundred men out there
who think that women should not even be
in a position like this, so we cannot afford
to be adequate; we must be exceptional—
clip, clop, clip, clop, clip, clop—"Cheryl,
where do you style your hair"—why
aren't you a model?—"That's Cheryl,
the slave-driver, don't talk to her"—"I
heard that Cheryl sucked his"—ringgggg!
Ringggggggggggggggggggg!*

– 4 –

"I take the subway because it's fuel
efficient and I'm a believer in sustainable
energy," Cheryl said. The doors slid shut.

"It's just that I couldn't imagine a girl
like you on one of these."

"Harold, that's impolite," the old
woman told him.

"I want a divorce," Harold said.

"Awww, shut up," the old woman said.

"It's alright with me, ma'am," Cheryl
said. She smiled. "It's a good question."

"You look like one of those models for
the lingerie company," Harold said.

"Please, Harold!" The old woman
rammed her heel in to his shoe.

"Well, before I worked in Fashion, I was
a model," Cheryl said. "It turns out, there's
more money behind the scenes than in the
pictures."

"And more food, too," Harold said.

"Yes, that too," Cheryl smiled. "Here's
my stop. It's been lovely talking to you." She
nodded, and stepped out into the street.

– 5 –

"Are you through," Cheryl asked.

"Go right ahead," the woman replied.
She wore a pink sweater and a yellow hat.
"I think it's the last of the small carts. I had
to go around the block for this one and pull
it off the corner. Otherwise I end up filling
up my cart with nothing but chocolate." She
laughed. "And cake!"

Cheryl smiled.

She went through the aisles.

*The goddamn wheel. It's clanking.*

"Hey," the woman said.

Cheryl looked back. The woman was
standing very close behind her. She held the
yellow hat in her hand.

"You ever been to the Midwest?"

"What?"

"I know you have."

"How do you know that?"

"You think you're so goddamn fancy
in your little outfit," she said. "But I know
who's fucking your husband."

"I'm sorry. What?"

"I know who is fucking your husband.
And it isn't you."

"Who are you?" Cheryl asked.

The woman's eyes got wider, and wider,
and wider. They were clouded with fear. And
the more afraid the woman looked, the more
afraid Cheryl felt.

– 6 –

Express Check-out. 15 items or less.

Tofu, almond milk, quinoa, kale, lean
ground turkey, yams, blueberries, egg whites.

"How are you today," Cheryl asked.

The man checking out her groceries just
looked at her.

– 7 –

"People are just not socially tactful," Cheryl said. "It's like their parents never taught them any manners."

"He works as a checkout guy. What do you think? He's going to be as high on life as you?"

"Well, it's not about that. It's about being smart. You know, you need to earn your way up. By being socially skilled."

"Babe—I think you got a little cellulite going on."

Cheryl looked down at her legs.

"I'll hit the gym tomorrow," she said. "It's my day off."

"That's my girl."

"That's right."

"I'm sorry?"

"This woman in the store. She told me that…she told me…"

"What was that, Cheryl?"

"I'm sorry…" Cheryl brushed past Stephen and went into the bathroom.

"The alcohol. It's turned over again. Stephen, you haven't been going through my things?"

"I never tread on that territory," Stephen said, with his hands in the air.

Chery dropped a paper towel on the floor.

It turned grey.

– 8 –

"Eugenia," Cheryl said. "You're fired."

– 9 –

Sometimes, when Stephen was asleep, Cheryl opened up her laptop and looked at the personal ads on Craigslist.

M4F.

*Looking For a Friend Who Still Sees the Stars*

*Hi. I don't know why I'm writing this. Most likely, if you're here, you're curious. Even more likely is that you're lonely. Well, I'm curious and lonely too. Why don't we chat?*

– 10 –

Cheryl began to type:

*Hi my name is*

She stopped. Stephen turned in his sleep. She closed her laptop.

– 11 –

The next evening, the subway ride back home was quiet. An old woman and an old man sat across from her. She smiled at them, and the man said, "What, ya cunt?"

Cheryl came home and set down her purse. She went into the bathroom. Her heels caught on the wet floor. Her head almost slammed in to the tub. She caught herself on her palms.

She heard the cabinet snap open and shut in the kitchen.

"Stephen," she said. "Stephen. God damn it, did you spill my alcohol on the floor?"

The phone rang.

– 12 –

"Hey babe. I won't be home till late tonight. You ok?"

"Yeah, babe."

"Don't forget to hit the gym."

"Yes."

Cheryl hung up the phone.

The windows were shut. There was no wind.

– 13 –

She turned on all the lights. She took a beer out of the fridge.

"Too many calories," she muttered.

She sat down and poured herself a glass of rye. She drank it. She opened her laptop. On the toolbar, there was a tab open. She pulled it up.

– 14 –

*Hi. I won't tell you who I am, or what I do. But I want you to know a little bit about me. I'm beautiful. Not like, to catfish you. It's a part of my job. And believe me, it's a curse more than a gift. I remember when I was in the first grade, a little boy told me that I looked like a giraffe. He said that I should eat leaves, and he shoved them all in my mouth. The point that I'm making is that it's not that great to be different than most people. And I am. Wow. I've already written a small essay, here. I guess I don't feel qualified to answer your ad. I don't see the stars. Not past all that smog. I wonder if I ever could.*

– 15 –

At work, a notification arrived on her cell. She pulled it open.

*If you measure beauty by the way they write, then you are beautiful, even to me. Hello stranger. What I am looking for is perhaps a bit unorthodox. I want someone to write to. I can't meet up with you at this juncture, for personal reasons. Now, indulge me for a little Q and A? No incriminating information, of course.*

– 16 –

Cheryl dropped her phone, and caught it with her pointed shoes.

She bent over and picked it up again.

– 17 –

*Hit me with your best shot.*

– 18 –

Cheryl sprayed the disinfectant on the cardio machine. She scrubbed it down with a white towel. A man across from her smiled. She smiled back, and ran on the machine.

– 19 –

*Romantic or Pragmatic?*

*Both. And you?*

*That means you're just pragmatic. A romantic would say "pragmatic," only. A cynic would say "romantic." If you say both, you're just a pragmatist.*

*How do you know that?*

*Because it's diplomatic. Isn't that what pragmatists are all about? And I won't answer the question. But I'll ask you a new one. Stones or the Beatles?*

*Oh. That's a no brainer. The Stones. I mean, come on.*

*Nirvana or Queen?*

*Neither.*

*Whaaaaaaaaaaaaa—I have no words. Are you insane*

*Ok, I like Freddie Mercury as a person. But something about his music reminds me of barbecues with burnt chicken and sweaty old white men in Hawaiian shirts...*

*Galileo! Galileo!*

*Ok.*

*There was a poor boy—in a poor—*

*OKAY.*

*Alright. Here's a question for you. Why did you answer my ad?*

– 20 –

"That's a Cheryl question," Stephen said. "She's got amazing communication skills."

"Yes, Sandra," John said. "Listen to Stephen's wife."

"Yes, speaking up is key," Cheryl said. "But so is precision. When you go into the boardroom, you have to monitor everything about yourself. But you have to appear effortless. Jewel toned clothing, to bring out your eyes. But not too bright. For you, maybe an emerald green. A suit jacket over that. Black pumps, but keep the heel to a minimum. Enough to accentuate your body, but not enough to go to the club. Make sure your hair is down, but out of your face. For your makeup…this smoky eye, it's good, but not working in your favor. Make it look like you aren't wearing any at all. Men love to see a woman 'without makeup.' That's just code for wearing mattes and nudes. And when you get out there, make sure you really speak. Don't say anything too self-serving. Make it clear that you're a team player, and that you're not afraid."

"Wow," Sandra said. "Wow, you really know what you're talking about."

"She's eighteen," John whispered.

"Oh!" Cheryl looked at Sandra's glass of wine, and then at John. "Oh," she said again.

"You're just so beautiful, Cheryl. I wish I could have hair like yours."

"That's very sweet," Cheryl said. "If you want, I can book you with my stylist."

"Johnny," Sandra smiled. "Johnny, doesn't that sound good?"

"Yes, well, you just got your hair done."

– 21 –

"You're looking sexy," Stephen said. "A little too sexy." He pulled on her shirt. He pulled it down. "Wow," he said. "Wow."

"Baby, I'm kind of…" Cheryl said.

"That red bra…is it new?"

"I guess so."

"How come you never showed it to me?"

"I guess I've just been busy."

"But here we are…at a hotel…far from home…with nothing to do…"

"Actually, I was thinking I would…" He stripped her down.

– 22 –

1 – 2 – 3 – 4 – 5 – 6 – 7 – 8 – 9 – 10.

"Ooooo. Ohhhhhh. Mmmm-Oh, Oooo!"

*Tomorrow, six o'clock. Dinner with the Forbes couple. Eight thirty. The gym. Nine thirty. Face mask. Hair restoration mask. Don't forget to tell Trish to call Isaac Newman to follow up on the new Spring line.*

"I'm coming! I'm coming!"

"Ooooo. Uhhhh. Mmmmmm. You go, baby, you come," Cheryl said.

– 23 –

Cheryl was in line at the store.

Vodka, tonic water, dark chocolate, paper towels, bleach, rice crackers, lentils, salmon, figs, kefir, almonds, cashews, low-fat ricotta, brown rice, apple cider vinegar, and a muffin. She looked at the muffin for a moment. *I cannot eat this.*

The same man worked at the store that she had seen a week ago.

"Ma'am, you have sixteen items here, and this is a fifteen item line."

"But sir…I'm not sure I understand."

"What don't you understand about this? Get into a different line."

"But no one has ever…"

"Read the sign. It says, fifteen items. You have sixteen items."

The woman in the pink sweater and yellow hat stood behind her.

"Please," she said. "Just hurry up and move already. I need to get my chocolate. And cake!"

– 24 –

Stephen was working late.

Cheryl sat down in bed and leaned into her hands.

The kitchen cabinet snapped open and shut.

– 25 –

She got up. She looked over the entire living room. The pictures were in place. She looked at herself in the mirror. Her eyes were afraid. She turned away. Her purse was on the counter. The vodka was on the counter. An orange was on the counter. She went into her bedroom and shut the door.

– 26 –

*More questions for me, sir?*

– 27 –

He didn't answer.

– 28 –

She went out into the apartment again. Everything was as it had been. The vodka was on the counter. An orange was on the counter. Her purse…was on the floor.

"Stephen," she said. "Stephen?"

– 29 –

Her heart pounded. She went to the phone and dialed Stephen's work. He picked up.

"I'm scared," she said. "I know you don't believe that he's real. I know you think it's some kind of psychological issue. But Stephen. Things are moving around the house without me touching them."

"Oh, babe, come on. Take a deep breath. Ok? And then exhale. Remember the rhythm I taught you."

"You know how anal retentive I am," she said. "God, Stephen. It's me. I have your entire wardrobe color coordinated. I know the layout of this house like the back of my hand. I know that things are being moved around this apartment. And Stephen…I get this feeling. Like he is listening to me. Like, right now."

"Sweetheart, I've been hesitant to say this, because I know how you feel about therapists."

"No. That's not happening."

"Have you ever considered…"

"They just tell you something is wrong with you. They don't think anything you experience is real. They just tell you to do cognitive behavioral therapy and call it a day."

"You really benefitted from that cognitive behavioral therapy last time. You were thinking much more rationally afterwards."

Cheryl jumped. Her work cell vibrated.

"I…I gotta go," she said.

*– 30 –*

*Tell me what your favorite book is?*

*Hello. You're back. Good. I almost wish I could ask you over. I'm terrified.*

*What are you scared of? Maybe I can talk you through it.*

*When you were a kid, did you ever have an imaginary friend?*

*I did.*

*Well, so did I. His name was Cheshire, like the cat in* Alice in Wonderland. *It was my favorite story as a kid. I had a really overactive imagination back then. It was so extreme that my mom told me that instead of playing with the other little girls, I would sit alone in my room and imagine things. I thought up stories. And my curiosity was insatiable. For everything. I dreamed of pirates, and musketeers, and bandits in black masks. I went to fairy-lands, and caves, and castles. And everything I dreamed, I wrote down. I drew pictures. I did it all on my father's printer paper. But after a while, it got lonely. So I invented Cheshire.*

*Ok.*

*And Cheshire. He was beautiful. The most beautiful boy you could imagine. He had big eyes, and a mischievous smile. He could backflip. He could juggle. He could climb almost anything. And then, one day, something went terribly wrong. It was after I turned twelve. He began to go through changes. I was getting more and more bullied in school, and I just stopped going. I would stay home and spend all of my time with Cheshire. And then. Oh my God. I'm so afraid. I wish you were here.*

*I am there in spirit.*

*Thank you. Are you reading all of this carefully?*

*Yes. Continue.*

*One day, he took everything I had ever written or drawn or colored. He swallowed and ate them. All of my paintings. All of my stories. Everything from before. It was gone. And the next day, I woke up next to him. And that face. Oh, God. It makes me sick. He was like nothing I've ever seen. He was something worse than a man or a monster. He was more powerful than anything else. A creature. Do you understand?*

*I think so.*

*And after that...oh my god, I told Cheshire, I said, "Get away from me." And that was when my trouble started.*

*What kind of trouble?*

*He would try to scare me. At first, it was innocent. He would pop up in the mirror while I brushed my teeth. He would wait on the other side of the shower curtain. Sometimes, he would just move my shoes, an inch to the left, so that I barely noticed anything was wrong. But I feared for my life. One day, when I got home from school, Cheshire got a knife from the kitchen and cut up my forearms. He told me it would look like a suicide.*

*And then?*

*And then my mom took me to a psychotherapist. That woman told me that I had an overactive imagination, and that I had to start connecting to other children.*

*Did you?*

*Oh, yes. I threw all of my books and movies into the trash. I replaced them with lipstick and hair curlers and perfume. I became the most popular girl in school. The most powerful. By the end of high school, I could get any of the boys to do anything for me.*

*And were you happy?*

*What?*

*Without your books. Without your*

*imagination. Were you happy?*

*Yes.*

*You hesitated.*

*No. I just wanted to answer honestly.*

*I know you're not being honest, Cheryl.*

– 31 –

Cheryl shot up out of bed. She wondered how she could just hear it before. The sound of hands against a keypad. The sound of breathing. She opened her bedroom door. Out there, on the couch, Cheshire sat. Cheryl nearly collapsed, but she was held by his gaze. He laughed. She tried to speak, but her voice would not come.

– 32 –

"You're not happy," he said. "I can see it in your eyes. Your husband is fucking someone else, and you know it. But you don't care about that. Do you? You don't care because you can't feel. You can't feel a thing. At night, when he takes you, you recite your schedule to yourself."

"I am happy," Cheryl said. "I am strong."

Cheshire laughed.

He began to scream, and then cry. "My name is Cheryl," he wept. "My name is Cheryl and I'm *unhappy*."

Cheryl turned around. The front door opened.

Stephen stood there.

"Baby," he said. "What is it? Did you see him again?"

She ran to him and held on tight.

"No," she whispered. "I just miss you. Can you hold me, hold me tight?"

"Cheryl. Of course."

He took her to the couch and cradled her on his lap. She fell asleep there, holding on to him.

– 33 –

"I don't believe in therapy, and I don't want to be here."

"Thank you for your candor," Selma replied. "I hope to give you a different experience than you have had before. And maybe, you'll benefit from having someone on your side."

Cheryl threw back her hair and crossed her legs.

"I don't have a side," she said. "I'm neutral."

"What did you want to talk about?"

"This is going to sound stupid," she said. "And I don't want you to tell me it's all in my head. They all say that, you know. They all say that."

"I will not invalidate you."

"I see someone. He's a monster."

"How long have you been seeing him?"

"Since I was a kid, not at all. But then, a couple weeks ago…it started."

"So, he's from your past."

"Yes. And he's following me."

"Do you know what he wants?"

"Not exactly. But when I look at him, I feel as though he wants to kill me."

"How were you before? When you were a kid?"

"I was all alone. But in my imagination, I could do anything."

"Do you still feel you can do anything you want?"

"Well, sure."

"Do you miss it?"

"What?"

"Being a child?"

"I miss…" Cheryl stopped. She looked up at Selma. "Do you want to know what my worst fear is?"

"What is it?"

"My mom and my dad, they both married for convenience. They worked jobs that they hated. They died without ever really living at all. I remember that in the other worlds, the ones that I invented, I was…free. I was allowed to taste, to touch, to feel. And now…"

"Maybe this monster is back for a reason," Selma said. "Maybe he isn't here to hurt you. Maybe he is here to help you."

– 34 –

*Cheshire. Meet me in my room tonight.*

– 35 –

There was no response. Cheryl sat on the white blankets in a black dress. The tv tray held two glasses of red wine. She looked at the window and then at the door. At last, it creaked open, little-by-little. He looked in with his eyes, first. And smiled. She felt her whole body grow weak.

"Have a seat," she said. "Right here. Have some wine."

He sat there.

"I know what this is," he said. "This is where you try to destroy me, and you walk out that door feeling like you're on top of the world. Feeling like you control something."

"Cheshire," she said. "I'm going to tell you a story."

"Tell."

"It's hard for me, because I don't know much anymore. I haven't read a book in years. But Rome wasn't built in a day, was it? So I'll try. Once upon a time, there was a little girl. She was to inherit a beautiful kingdom. But, instead of learning how to dance, and what to wear, the little girl spent all of her time in the fields, playing with the fairies…"

Cheshire listened.

And as he listened, he grew smaller.

"Her parents told her, 'The real world won't do you any favors. If you don't stop those childish games, you'll never succeed.' So, she turned her back on childish things. That was when a trickster of fairy-land decided to take his revenge. He was so hurt that she had turned her back on him that he began to destroy everything in her path. He swore that she would never become queen. He was banished from the kingdom, but he told her, 'When you are of age, I will return, and I will make you my bride.'"

Cheshire was a child now. He looked up at Cheryl and tilted his head.

"And then what," he asked her.

"And then, he went away. But…" Cheryl stopped now. Cheshire lay down on her bed. His eyes had filled with tears.

"But she was never ok again. The real world was cold, and unfeeling, and dark. And slowly, the princess lost everything that ever meant anything to her. The taste of the sunset. The smell of the sea. The touch of someone against her. It felt like nothing now. She soon forgot the way that it felt to walk barefoot in the garden. And to dance in the wind. And to fall in love. It was as though she was a shadow, going through the mechanics of ruling a kingdom. But feeling nothing. Desiring nothing. Living as nothing."

"Did he come back for her?"

"He did. But by the time he did, she had forgotten all about the fairy kingdom. So she saw him, and was terrified. She thought that he wanted to kill her. And so she devised a plan. She would lure him to her side, and then kill him."

"What happened then?"

"He fell into her trap. He came to her chambers. And lay down on her bed, like you're lying on mine. So she leaned down, and she kissed his forehead." Cheryl leaned down, and kissed his.

"She said what I am about to say to you. I am sorry. I am sorry I lost my self, and turned my back on you. I am sorry I lived my life so empty. Like a dead woman walking."

"And how does it end," Cheshire asked.

"You have to make up the ending," Cheryl said. "Like we used to."

"Ok. In the end, the fairy prince realized that although he was the most elegant, and wonderful, and handsome, and delightful, and intelligent, and marvelous creature alive,"—Cheshire stood up and did a little flip on the bed—"he realized that he loved the princess more than anything in the world. He realized that in order to be happy he would have to make a sacrifice and give her something that would bring her back to life." Cheshire got up and went into the other room. He returned, a monster once more.

He held a kitchen knife.

Cheryl leaned back away from him and put her wrists behind her back.

"My queen," he whispered. He came closer. He leaned his face against hers. He took her hands out. "Show them to me," he said. She showed him.

"Please," she said. "The scars are still there."

He whispered to her, "Kiss me, and I'll become a prince."

Cheryl kissed the monster. When she released herself, she saw a man, as beautiful as the boy had been, but strong.

He took the knife and ran it from his throat to his stomach. His body fell apart as he crumbled to the floor. Pages unraveled out of his body and onto the ground. He became nothing but air.

Cheryl took the pages up into her hands, and ate them.

When she was through, she looked up from the floor, alone.

The apartment was well lit.

# MAMA IS ALWAYS ONSTAGE

## THOMAS KEARNES

For my mother

The checkered blindfold slipped down Hogan's nose. Kneeling before a Latino man, he tried to concentrate. The swarthy man's hips bopped closer to his face. Hogan fretted upon hearing the man's heavy, irritated sigh. The blindfold fell from his eyes, but his lids were shut tight.

Hogan liked to please unseen men, at least once a week, sometimes more. Their approval, these beneficiaries of what Hogan promised, allowed him to believe the homosexuals of Dallas accepted him. All it cost was his dignity. He'd first offered another man blind pleasure, at the same bathhouse, almost twenty years ago.

"I'm sorry," Hogan finally said, grabbing the blindfold from the concrete floor. "I can still suck you off."

"You're sweet." The Latino man backed toward the door. "But I check out soon." Before Hogan had begun servicing him, the man mentioned his recent arrival; he had hours before checkout time. Hogan didn't mind the white lie. He was grateful the man

spoke at all. Most didn't.

Hogan's knees ached. Chugging two caps of GHB now seemed unwise. Sex filled the void quickly, the bottomless shaft of self-loathing inside him. Sometimes the shame, paired with the ecstasy, was so overwhelming that he remained limp.

He left the door wide open, inviting men to behold how he stroked himself closer to release. An attendant announced over a loudspeaker that room 325 needed attention. Hogan groaned with pleasure. He planned to delay climax until someone could watch.

He didn't hear the knock.

"Need some help with that?"

Hogan didn't want to stretch back and turn. Manners, though, demanded he meet the stranger's gaze. His new guest was certainly middle-aged: hair almost fully gray, jowls forming, lengthy crinkles fanning out from the corners of his eyes. The bottom of his ass collapsed into a series of wrinkles. Before Hogan uttered a welcome, the man stepped closer, slapping his hand over his fist and making a popping sound with his mouth—casual, keep it casual. But he stopped. His brow bunched in confusion, and he wrapped his arms around himself.

Hogan hoped his impish belly, scattered gray chest hair and bags beneath his eyes didn't disappoint. He'd turned forty last month. He'd spent his birthday on his knees.

"What's wrong?" Hogan asked.

"Don't you feel that?"

"I can't feel anything."

"It must be fifty degrees in here."

Hogan chuckled. "You got some bad shit, handsome."

"I'm serious." The man spun around, arms folded. He glanced over his shoulder. "Come to 313. We'll smoke some dope and do naked things. Too damn cold in here." The man left. His offer to hook up in his room hadn't registered with Hogan. The Latino man's earlier rejection had soured his perception. He had enough dope for another bowl.

"My Lord, child, there's not enough room in here to change your mind." The voice was high and melodious, an ice cream truck on an August afternoon, the bells of a rushing sleigh.

*Not tonight*, he thought. *I just wanted to suck strangers.*

It was not the first time Mama had come to visit.

"Does this door lock? I don't want one of your friends barging in." She fiddled with the knob. It clicked, and Mama hooted, triumphant.

"You're not real."

"Don't sass me." She tapped her foot. The steel plate attached to her shoe banged and echoed through the tiny room. Since her first appearance the day after Christmas, Mama always wore her taps, oblivious to the sharp *pops* exploding with each step.

"You're not my mother."

"I can't imagine who else could stomach the way you slut around."

He rubbed his temples, turned his back. Mama, however, would not vanish. She always appeared with hair frosted to hide the gray. She wore a sequined white dinner jacket, red bow tie and dark slacks. Her dance team, comprised of other middle-aged ladies, from long ago had worn the same outfit.

Hogan blew a sinister bank of smoke, hoping it would demolish the illusion. She waved her hands dramatically until the smoke dissipated. "Was that supposed to impress me?" Her curt tone indicated it had not.

"I can't talk right now."

"All these bad choices...we need to talk, honey."

He smirked. "That ship has sailed, Mama."

Her spooky violet eyes narrowed. She pointed her finger, shaking it in his face. "You were always a quitter. Boy Scouts, football, so many jobs...."

"Then leave before I disappoint you again."

"Still got a smart mouth."

"Come back when I'm not tweaked, okay?"

She looked stricken. "I can't wait that long."

*Wait*, he thought, *how does she know what* tweaked *means?*

She tried the door, and then shook her head, smiling at her own foolishness. She'd forgotten locking it, Hogan figured. He exhaled loudly and stepped toward her. Mama stopped him with a hand raised to his chest. "I locked it myself. I'll unlock it myself." Stepping around her, he jiggled the knob. The door swung open.

"My Hogie, such a capable boy." He froze when she kissed his forehead, stayed motionless as she stepped out of the room, metallic pops at first loud, but already fading. His heart raced. *Ghosts can't touch you*, he thought. She hadn't before. After a deep breath, he peered into the hall. Mama was gone.

*Mama breaks from the line of women to perform her solo. She taps and tilts, arms stretched like the wings of a single-jet airplane. Lights bounce off her sequins, dazzling the crowd. Tap, tap, and* smile! *Tap, tap, and* grin! *The boys and girls don't hide their derision; rolled eyes and snickers tempt their teachers' open hands.*

*One boy, younger than the others, his back against the wall, stands mesmerized. Mama is so young and arresting, chestnut locks spinning as she reaches the finale. The spotlight shines down like the Arizona sun, but Mama keeps her eyes wide. The boy's eyes are the same eerie violet.*

*Followed by the troupe, Mama strikes a pose before a flourish of strings. Mama doesn't lose her smile as her shoulders heave. The teachers gesture for the children to clap—or else. The boy with violet eyes pounds his palms together till they hurt. Mama winks at him. He is five years old. Mama loves the boy—it is certain like the sunrise.*

Kyle rarely arrived early. Hogan thought he had more time to disguise his latest binge. He showered, brushed his teeth for five whole minutes to compensate for the skipped days, shaved, and then poured Visine into his eyes. Naked and nervous in the bathroom, he heard a knock downstairs. He'd hoped to exclude Trevor from his afternoon with Kyle, but his housemate's bedroom window overlooked the front entrance.

"Baby," Hogan barked to at the neighboring room. "See who it is."

After a moment came the reply. "It's the ungrateful shit."

"Let him in. I'm not dressed."

Kyle knocked again, louder. "Hogie, you there?" he called.

"I refuse to do that boy a single favor," Trevor said.

"I explained all that," Hogan said. "He didn't mean it."

"He didn't mean his apology, neither."

Hogan scurried to his bedroom, tossed on a hooded sweatshirt and pulled on faded jeans. "Baby, it's freezing outside." It was easier to do it himself than persuade Trevor. They'd split six months ago. Both men lacked the funds to abandon their townhouse, bought in a haze of optimism and love. More importantly, Hogan wasn't ready to concede failure and live alone.

Barefoot, Hogan threw open the door, his arms open wide. Kyle shuffled into his embrace but didn't return it. Before scuttling into his teen years, Kyle had hugged Hogan with a ferocity that made him wish for children of his own. Hogan released him, catching his face.

Acne feathered the teen's forehead. He'd pierced his left ear a sixth time. A kidney-shaped bruise lurked on his upper throat. A rush of desire filled Hogan, a desire to show his godson the entire world, its wonders and winters. All he hoped were that girls, not boys, had left their marks on Kyle. He wouldn't wish his life, even his expired heyday with Trevor, on anyone, let alone a child who loved him.

"Let's get out of here," Kyle said.

Kyle's fondness for fast food offered Hogan a respite from the pretentious bistros and cafés swarming Oak Lawn, the city's gay nexus. He feigned indecision, but he'd known what he wanted long before pulling into the Whataburger lot.

"Mom wants me to ask you a question," Kyle said, Hogan taking a bite from his burger.

"Why not ask me herself?"

"If you put up half the cost, Mom will match it. I'll finally have some wheels."

Hogan swallowed before he'd finished chewing. He coughed and sucked down soda. He hated telling Kyle no. Often truant and unabashedly fond of marijuana, Kyle didn't need an automobile making these vices shimmer even more seductively. Hogan sighed and raised his brows, pretended to consider it. Kyle rolled his eyes, grimacing. That's when Hogan saw him.

The boy was still in high school, no older than Kyle. Blond hair spilled down his neck, all but the ends hidden by a Rangers cap. A gray sleeveless tee showcased his biceps, their thickness incongruent with his tall, slender frame.

"Do you feel that?" Kyle said, rubbing his bare arms.

"What?" Hogan didn't look at Kyle.

"It got real fucking cold real fucking fast."

The passing boy glared at Hogan with such naked hostility, he wondered if *faggot* was stenciled on his forehead. Still, his gaze followed the faun-like specimen slouching past.

He then sat across from Mama.

The color drained from Hogan's face.

His hands balled into fists. Despite being born after her death, Kyle might see her; he'd probably never noticed her framed photos in the townhouse. Silence fell. Kyle bit his burger as if Mama weren't there. She would not look at Hogan. Surely, she knew he watched her. Surely, he would see her again.

"Try not to hit the pipe with some random dude before you decide."

Hogan jerked back in his seat. *Everybody knows*, he thought. *They knew before me.*

"I have to think about it."

"Would a blowjob convince you?"

Hogan's voice hardened. "Don't joke like that."

"If I was joking, you'd be laughing."

When they said goodbye, Kyle offered Hogan his hand. Hogan sadly shook it, wished him a early happy birthday, receiving no thanks. He'd turn seventeen next week. Hogan slumped beside the door, watched him drift into the chilly night. Before he settled into this emotional purgatory downstairs, Trevor announced from upstairs that Meredith waited on the land line.

"Why not call my cell like everyone else?"

"I like to set myself apart," Meredith said. "You know that."

"Before he tells you, I said I would think about it."

"Think about what?"

"Getting him a car."

"Fucking hell. That's just what I need."

"This wasn't your idea?"

Meredith's piercing cackle mocked Hogan. Of course he was susceptible to Kyle's schemes; only a real father could smell his son's *bullshit*.

Hogan and Meredith had met in an undergraduate art class over two decades ago, before he'd first put on a blindfold. They'd studied figure drawing; a dumb freshman boy posed on a stool. His chin rested upon his hand and his right thigh dipped, revealing a greater gift than most men could claim. Hogan was no artist. The professor, though, had been so encouraging that dropping the course seemed rude. He'd gazed in wonder at the model. It hadn't been until Meredith giggled that he realized his frank admiration drew its own stares. Both had felt an instant kinship.

They'd met for coffee, scoped out men in bars, held each other through the tears following break-ups. He was the only one Meredith would trust with her child. As Kyle neared manhood, however, Hogan noticed a stirring within himself that would shatter their friendship forever.

"Baby," she said, "please tell me you didn't need me to figure that out."

"I was just keeping you informed."

"Sure, Hogie." Over the line, he heard ice clink against a glass. At least she *sounded* sober. "That boy always gets you to grab your ankles."

"Your little jokes are worse than his."

"I'll burst his bubble on your behalf."

"Tell him I wanted to say yes."

"With that boy, it's the only word you know."

Hogan blushed. He prayed that Meredith never deduced how badly he desired the boy to confide in him. "Maybe he won't be too pissed…."

Upstairs, Trevor slammed his bedroom door and stomped into the bathroom. Another slam. Hogan knew his ex-lover's route to perfection. Strung out so many nights on the downstairs sofa, he'd listened to his past lumber overhead.

After the call, Hogan sat on the sill of their picture window, gazing into the starless night. Even with the cloudbanks drifting past, the moon shone through like an unwanted truth. He tried not to follow the thumps and bangs upstairs.

Trevor rarely lacked male company. At first, Hogan was glad to see his ex-lover "moving on," the phrase absurdly inadequate to describe this separation stagnating under one roof. Hogan had tacit permission to do the same. Still, nights not spent with Kyle and Meredith or lurking the dank bathhouse halls found him listless against the window, wishing he were invited into the blackness. He debated opening the window, letting the cold blast him.

The prolonged silence upstairs spooked him. Trevor would soon leave and Hogan would miss him—this was the routine.

*Mama's hair doesn't spin madly anymore. She hacked it off. Raising a child alone, she says. No damn time for silliness. She finds time to dance, however, the staccato beats from her taps bouncing through the auditorium like calls across a canyon. Still, the children giggle and roll their eyes. Still, the teachers resist their urge to smack a brat—that's what children need.*

*She dances another solo. Every year, another solo. Arms wide, her fingers tickle the air. Tap, tap and smile! Tap, tap and grin! A savior's fervor flashes in her violet eyes. The children watch without comprehension; at their age, they believe such passion to be a rare and good thing. One day, the teachers sadly must inform them otherwise.*

*The boy is growing older, growing taller. He is secretly pleased to be among the class arriving last, stuck in the back row, the coffin-sized speakers booming and crackling behind him. A blond boy slips him a baseball card featuring a lesser-known player from a lesser-known team. Worthless, guaranteed to attract no serious collector. The boy, however, plucks from his pocket his most treasured card. The blond boy's face reminds him of an unwrapped lollipop: sweet, immense and endlessly his to explore. The boy with violet eyes would've traded all the men in his deck for one grin from that blond boy.*

*Mama stomps the linoleum stage, her shoes banging like a god's promise. She and the other dancers lift their arms as a cacophony of horns washes over them. The children applaud, including the boy. He doesn't clap as passionately as he did when smaller; the blond boy might award him the sort of attention no child wants. Mama winks at him. He is nine years old. Mama loves the boy—it is certain like the sunrise.*

Trevor rushed about, packing for a one-week trip to Fiji. Hogan wanted to offer help, to assure him that it wasn't *at all* spooky how a random guy had invited him out of the country after a wild weekend at the bathhouse. I have a good feeling about him, Trevor had informed his ex-lover. He'd then rhapsodized for ten whole minutes about Warner's sly smile, toned physique and...other attributes. Hogan had tried not to weep. He tried still.

"Baby, you got a spare box of rubbers? I'm not going out in this cold."

"Since when do you suit up for battle?"

"He'll think I'm a whore. He'll think I have diseases."

"You don't know the first fucking thing about this guy."

"I knew *everything* about you." Trevor

stuffed a wad of black bikini briefs into his bag. "And look what it got me: a house I'm desperate to leave and my ex sleeping in the next room."

"I'm sorry, baby."

Trevor held up a silk turquoise pajama set, inspected it. Hogan recalled the first night Trevor slid into their bed, the sleeve of his top slipping over Hogan's waist. Don't strip me bare too soon, Trevor had cooed. You don't need me naked to feel good. Hogan's eyelids fluttered, and it took him a moment to notice Trevor waiting.

"You look great in that," Hogan said.

"I look even better out of it." Trevor shrugged one shoulder and folded the garments crisply, like a retail veteran. "Before I forget, I'd rather you not call me that." His cold gaze startled Hogan. "We've discussed this before. I'm not your baby."

Hogan watched his ex-lover select Birkenstocks over shiny black loafers. He watched him jam three Dean Koontz paperbacks into the duffel bag, their corners stretching the vinyl fabric. He watched him pluck a bottle of cologne from the nightstand, said nothing even though it wasn't his. Trevor stopped folding a pinstripe shirt and scolded his ex-lover. "Stop it, you're creeping me out."

"I thought...what do—?"

"Staring a hole through my head won't bring me back."

"This guy could be crazy," Hogan said.

"I survived you, didn't I?"

"I'm serious."

"I know, I know. You're always serious." Trevor threw down his shirt and *stormed* out. Hogan knew to perfection these righteous parades between rooms. Always, though, he feared Trevor wouldn't return. He sped after him.

Trevor charged down the stairs, Hogan on his heels. But Trevor's next announcement stopped him cold. "After Fiji, I'm looking for my own place." Hogan's face collapsed—so much for living in a house he couldn't leave. "Don't pretend you're surprised."

The staircase yawned before Hogan. Every step would bring him closer to the man who'd thoughtlessly changed his fate yet again. He despised himself for bestowing that power upon Trevor. He'd let Kyle exert a similar influence over him. And the men hidden by his blindfold, he couldn't forget them....

"You can't do that."

Trevor paused, gripping the banister. "I'll make this month's payment."

"Baby, please—"

"Don't call me that!"

"Where are you going?" Hogan ventured onto the top stair. He tried to think, but all he envisioned was another lonely night in a rented room, the blindfold slipping down his nose. His choices—Mama had wanted to discuss his bad choices.

Hogan descended, and but Trevor zipped across the room. "To Fiji. Try to keep up."

"We've sunk too much money into this place." His heart pounded, his palms clammy. "I can't afford this house alone."

Trevor's face softened and his shoulders fell. Hogan's breath caught with absurd optimism. He didn't hear the downstairs phone ringing until Trevor withdrew from the staircase, his ex-lover's optimism proven foolish, and disappeared into the living room.

"You could always shack up with *Lady Lush*," Trevor called out.

Hogan listened to Trevor answer the phone. Meredith liked to flirt with Trevor despite his disdain for her son, or perhaps it was because of that. He attempted to extract himself from the conversation. Sensation returned to Hogan's feet, and he hurried to the phone. Trevor passed him the receiver. "Drunk bitch is no longer my problem."

"Have you seen Kyle?" she asked.

"What do you mean?"

Kyle enjoyed making Hogan and his mother fret. At least, Meredith thought so. Hogan hoped his godson's motives were less sinister. Each time she called to report her son's disappearance, Hogan initially believed her mistaken—she was drunk; he was joking; she was paranoid.

Hogan checked to see if Trevor was eavesdropping. He relaxed to find his ex-lover gone. Footsteps clomped over his head. His gaze lifted to the ceiling, following Trevor's path.

"I'm panicking," she said. "That's what the little shit wants."

"That's right." Hogan's tone was flat. "It's a head game. That's all."

"Jesus, Hogan!" Trevor shouted from upstairs. Hogan clamped his hand over the mouthpiece. Meredith knew how badly Trevor mistreated him—the fights, the insults, the silences. Still, Hogan protected him. Trevor was still a dear friend, he often said. "Call the fucking repairman tomorrow," Trevor demanded. "It's colder upstairs than it is outside. Goddamn furnace."

"Where are you?" Trevor called to the ceiling.

"You said you had condoms, right?"

Meredith's voice seeped through Hogan's fingers. He'd let himself be distracted, and for longer than just this phone call.

"Baby," Hogan said. "I'm sorry. You there?"

"I don't know why I give shit…" She was crying.

"He's your son. Of course you—"

The horrible click, followed by a hum, jolted him. Meredith had never simply hung up. You lose, you lose, you lose—the losses pile up, but they do not cease, they cannot be stopped.

"Hogan, what the fuck is this?!?"

Trevor rushed downstairs, gripping a small stack of glossy photos. His eyes bulged with fury. Hogan couldn't process all this malevolence. *How could the furnace blink out so suddenly*, he wondered mildly. It had been toasty when he'd watched Trevor pack.

"You're a sick fuck," Trevor cried as he finished the stairs. "I should've known, you wanting to take that twink home from the club last year."

"What are you talking about? What are those?"

Trevor shoved the photos into Hogan's chest. Hogan didn't look at the pictures; they fluttered to the floor. "Look at them, pervert."

"Baby, what's wrong?"

Trevor grabbed Hogan by the throat, and he finally understood: they were not lovers, not friends, not housemates—at least, not for long. He was an inconvenience and not one bit more.

"You will *never* call me that again."

"Where did those come from?"

"Spare me the shit, Hogan."

Hogan stooped to the floor, collecting the photos He didn't know their subject. Trevor remained tall and erect before him; Hogan quietly wondered whether his housekeeping skills were in doubt. Finally, he glimpsed one of the images.

Mama had never looked so beautiful.

Trevor snorted, "Can't get enough, can you, pervert?"

In one photo, Mama held an infant to her breast. She was young, eyes bright with possibility, no older than twenty-five. Despite her stage makeup and white sequined jacket, she cradled the infant boy delivered into her arms. To Hogan's knowledge, no such photo existed; neither did the next one he studied.

"You gettin' hard, sicko?" Trevor sneered.

This image captured Mama, in sunglasses and full dance attire, perched at the ledge of a pier, hand poised over her eyes to block the glaring sun. A violet-eyed boy splashed below in the rough waters. Sifting through these counterfeit memories, their immediacy crushed him. The muscles in his calves and thighs cramped, his stomach stirred, he forgot to inhale. After the fifth or sixth photo, Hogan realized Trevor was gone. Footsteps thundered up the stairs. He'd been so enveloped in a private agony that his ex-lover's disgust felt no less distant than the moon. The last photo featured an older Mama, a woman whose beauty had faded but still offered solace. As in every shot, she wore her dance attire, sequins sparkling. Here, her arm circled a teenage boy's waist. The young man wore a navy blue cap and gown; he beamed with pride. The young man must've been Hogan: violet eyes, full lips, cleft chin….

But it was not him—none of these boys were him. Impossible, for reasons he knew as intimately as the steps leading up to the room he once shared with Trevor, the same steps upon which Trevor now stomped, dragging his bag like a mewling child from a candy store.

"I'll send for my other shit later."

"Is this a…joke?" Hogan gripped the cache of photos, incredulous.

"I'm not living with that filth under my roof." At the door, Trevor fumbled with the locks, hands shaking. He dug in his pocket and flung a tiny bag of crystals at Hogan, like they were inept performers in a just-say-no campaign. "It was this and the fucking house, right? Trevor and Hogan! Together forever! Meth and a mortgage!" Regret soaked Trevor's voice, too much but not nearly enough.

After Trevor slammed the door behind him, Hogan consumed the baggie's contents in moments; the high throbbed inside him like he needed more than air. The photos of Mama and not-Hogan—he felt the urge to revisit their faux warmth.

Mama had vanished. Every last photo: gone. At least, those upon which he'd gazed…

Hogan recognized Kyle's bedroom at once: the bed too wide, the Green Day and Radiohead posters, the open closet revealing an army of sleeveless T-shirts. Meredith occasionally sent her friend to fetch Kyle if they weren't on speaking terms.

In the first photo, clenched in Hogan's hand, Kyle sat on the corner of his bed, legs spread wide, proud of what stood hard between his thighs. So…now Hogan knew. When tweaked, he'd wondered about Kyle's endowment. Kyle leered into the lens. One image followed another of provocative poses. Toward the end of the stack, a man fellated Kyle, his back to the lens and Kyle's face blank. Hogan flipped through the stack, trying to will the innocent (if impossible) shots of Mama to reappear.

*Such a beautiful boy*, he thought helplessly. *Such a beautiful man.*

The images tumbled from his hand.

The first set, the ones with Mama, had been meant for his eyes only. Kyle's lewd pictorial was intended for his viewing pleasure as well. At least, that's what he suspected. Trevor's discovery of the hardcore series was simply the latest in a lifetime of misfortunes.

*Mama nears her middle years but still dances with more panache than the others. Of course, she commands the attention of the grade-school children sitting grim and quiet like a dozen rows of industrious ants. The music hasn't changed: anonymous dance-pop all featuring some half-forgotten diva wailing the chorus at song's end, just in time for Mama to twirl and tap and pop her eyes like a lottery winner ambushed by a camera crew.*

*No true performer would seek out a particular audience member during a routine. It's unprofessional, a guaranteed distraction. Her eyes, however, lose a bit of brightness when she can't find her son. Tap, tap and* smile! *Tap, tap and* grin! *The children don't notice, or if they do, cannot comprehend the sting of loss a child inflicts on his mother every day until death.*

*Finally, they enter the auditorium, stand beside one another by a speaker. Mama worries about her son's hearing. Coach Fell has been so good to her and the boy. Reminded her she was a woman long before she was a mother. So good and kind of him to escort her boy to the performance. The boy's eyes dart nervously back and forth, leery of the children. Or the coach. But yes, definitely leery…*

*Mama's feet erupt in a series of staccato steps that remind the boy of an SOS signal. Help me, I'm dying. You're my only hope. He applauds, loud and deliberate, unsure whether the gesture is meant to appease Coach or Mama. Mama winks at him as the curtain closes. He is thirteen years old. Mama loves the boy—it is certain like the sunrise.*

Kyle studied his fingernails, his face slack. Hogan watched with both terror and desire. Loneliness plagued him with such tenacity that the smallest overture might push him over the cliff, headfirst into perversion.

"I have a tiny confession to make, Hogie."

"I'm listening."

"I planted those pictures."

Hogan swallowed, felt a granny knot slide down his throat, toward his gut. "They were for me, right? Early Christmas present?" He couldn't let the boy know he'd felt damned even before the boy's scheme unfolded.

"Why would *you* need to see them?" Kyle asked innocently. "Doesn't take a GPS to know you want my ass."

Hogan caught his drooping head, shook it in disbelief, hand over his eyes. Ten minutes earlier, Kyle had arrived unannounced, and Hogan welcomed him inside, not thinking once to call Meredith. Hogan had tried to shove under the sofa Kyle's lurid photos, but one had escaped him. The moment Kyle spied it, he'd invited Hogan to sit, Kyle taking a seat opposite him. There was no danger they might touch, Hogan told himself. He was the adult; he had to navigate, with precision, his desires along with Kyle's sinister motives. Alas, the meth retarded his faculties.

Finally, Hogan cleared his throat. "That's a long way to go for a cheap thrill."

"There's nothing cheap about that car I want."

"Do you have any idea how much shit I've gone through, in a single day?"

"Trevor was a hypocrite," Kyle said. "You can do better."

"What the fuck do you mean?"

His eyes darkened. He slid forward so quickly, like a cobra, Hogan feared he might strike. "He's been sucking my dick ever since you two hooked up."

Nearly eighteen months. Kyle would've been fifteen when Trevor had quickly swept Hogan past all prudence and sensibility. Hogan knew he must leave this room, let Kyle transform the first floor into his lair, anything so long as he can leave.

"He must've shown you only the photographs that didn't include him," Kyle mused. Hogan noticed a new tattoo, a small one on his inner forearm: a cross with ivy crawling upon it. "You were supposed to find them and freak out. Then, you'd threaten to show them to Mom and I'd squeeze whatever cash I needed from Trevor. Mom would think it came from you."

"Where are *those* pictures?" Hogan asked. "The ones including him?"

"Oh, yeah…" Kyle cackled. "I bet you'd like to watch him polish my apple, huh?"

He envied Kyle's cunning. His encounters with men might've been mere rebellion or a prelude to his adulthood sexual desires. Hogan sadly admitted to himself that a boy young enough to be his son had adroitly untangled a granny knot Hogan had found hopeless. Trevor had proven himself a cunning and devious man, to be sure. Hogan had never been a match for him. His gaze emptied, he simply listened to his godson recount his failed plot.

Kyle rose and picked up the remote.

He grinned at Hogan, a grin his godfather recognized all too well. "So how were you spending your busy Friday night?"

"Kyle, no, I need to—I didn't—"

"Let's watch some faggot remodel rich people's bathrooms. Mom loves Nate Berkus."

It was European porn, from one of Russia's new countries, in which a minimum age for performers was more suggestion than law. On the screen, a lithe blond boy penetrated a shorter, tan boy atop a workout bench. The music irritated, sounding distinctly Slavic.

"You're too young for this, Kyle."

"If I'm old enough to attempt extortion, I can handle overseas ass-pounding." Kyle drifted toward Hogan. "I brought a surprise." He produced from his messenger bag a black case small sized to carry eyeglasses. He lifted the glass pipe from the case and inspected the bowl.

"Thanks, I've had enough." Hogan pretended the teenage boys having sex onscreen completely absorbed him. "I promised your mother we'd never do that."

"But I never promised the reverse."

Kyle offered the pipe to Hogan, white smoke still trailing from the bowl. Hogan took it with the trepidation of a thirsty man reaching for an oasis. He wanted this. No one was there to say no. As Hogan drew in the smoke, Kyle slipped off his shirt. It dropped to the floor. Hogan exhaled onto Kyle's naked torso as it glistened hairless and tight. He kept his gaze focused there, terrified of meeting Kyle's eyes.

"What would happen if things were different?" Kyle asked.

"How?"

"If I wasn't your godson." Kyle dropped his jeans, revealed black thong underwear,

reserved only for the very young or very fit. "If I was just some trick from the bar." He guided Hogan's free hand to his crotch, manually manipulated the older man's fingers. "I could be anyone, Hogie. Your boyfriend told me all about your blindfold fetish."

Hogan yanked his hand away. He couldn't squelch the hurt and betrayal. His ex-lover had betrayed him in so many ways—Hogan felt a perverse urge to select a favorite. He demanded the remote from Kyle, but, perhaps sensing the shift in dynamics, Kyle instead knelt before him, arms crossed. He rested them atop Hogan's knees, his head tilted upward in mock surrender.

"Forget every other fucker. This is about me and you. I need a man. I need you, Hogie."

It was going to happen, Hogan thought. He was letting it happen. It had been so long since a man had wanted him, Hogan, and not just a willing orifice, that he succumbed. Kyle took him into his mouth, and Hogan leaned back, staring at the ceiling.

Kyle stopped. "No, I want you to watch me. Remember what I'm doing." Hogan obeyed. "One more thing," Kyle said. "Sing me 'Happy Birthday.' Mom's drunk. You're the only one who really cares." Hogan detected a note of sorrow in the boy's voice, but he was too aroused to realize this had been his godson's one moment of true vulnerability, at least for tonight.

Hogan began to sing, the notes sharp as pleasure surged through his body. He watched Kyle's head bob atop his lap. He glanced at the porn, and his brow clenched with bafflement.

The actors milled about, confused. They shivered, began to clutch one another for heat. If Kyle noticed their silence, he didn't let it interfere. From a doorway behind the actors, Mama emerged. She looked lost. She glanced once at the freezing, huddled actors. Her eyes still unfocused, seeming to recognize nothing, she stumbled past them. "Where's my son?" she asked the room. "Has anyone seen my son?" Hogan reached for the remote, but it lay too far away.

*Mama is tired. So many disappointments in love, false friends and fiendish rumors. She has decided this will be her last year to dance. Of course, the children do not know this. Likely, most will not notice her absence next year. Mama knows this, but it doesn't stop her. Tap, tap and* smile! *Tap, tap and* grin! *The choreographer picked a song especially for her. The Supremes' "Someday We'll Be Together." Mama dances with a renewed purpose, fingers straight like sabers, feet loose and powerful.*

*She looks for him in the audience. He would be hard to miss, an older boy among all these children. He looks more like his father every day; she never tells him this. Mama has danced so long that she can scan a crowd, face by face, and never miss a step. Surely, she thinks, he'll be here by curtain. He has his own car; coming and going as he pleases.*

*The boy and the track star he refuses to call his lover wallow naked in a bathtub full of bubbles. The bubbles were the boy's idea. The track star says he loves that about him— his spontaneity. He doesn't use the word* love, *of course, but he conveys the feeling. They ditched class and hustled to Mama's house. The track star wished to make love in every room, a sexual odyssey often suggested in soap operas and trashy novels.*

Not Mama's room, *the boy says.* Never

there. *The hours pass.*

*Mama winks at the audience as the curtain closes, just in case he's there and she missed him. Some of the children think the wink was for them. They giggle. They point. They hope they never become this crazy old woman in sequins and bow tie begging for children's applause.*

*The track star panics when he hears a pounding at the door. The boy instructs him to hide in his closet, and then he answers. The state trooper asks his name. He asks about Mama. Yes, she's my mother. The trooper gives the details of the accident. Does the boy have relatives who might come to stay? No, it's always been just me and Mama. After the trooper leaves, the boy flattens himself against the closed door. He can't breathe: so many routines, so many corny melodies, so many rude children. In his mind, Mama winks as the curtains close. He is seventeen years old. Mama loved the boy—it was certain like the sunrise.*

The checkered blindfold slid down Hogan's nose. He knew to replace it but had no clue about how to tell the difference between adequate blindfolds and defective ones.

The man currently thrusting himself between Hogan's lips was not a nice man. He'd flung the door all the way open, the *wham* spooking Hogan. This man liked poppers. Hogan had never understood the drug's minimal, transient allure. A steady succession of snorts overhead kept Hogan focused. The man had not asked his name, if he was tweaked, when he'd arrived.

"I know how much you want that, little bitch."

Hogan moaned his assent.

"Bet you can go twice with that mouth."

Coughing, Hogan jerked the man from his mouth. He was tired of playing the whore. He'd drafted his godson into that same role two hours ago. Upon climaxing and watching with dread as Kyle swallowed, Hogan rushed him from the house, thanking his godson for treating him so well, for telling the truth. At least, Kyle's most recent version of it.

The cash had fled his wallet as if by magic. Kyle looked at him, perplexed, the first point that evening, perhaps, in which matters hadn't followed his outline. Five hundred dollars, that's what Hogan shoved into the lovely boy's hand. I'll talk to your mother, he promised. Kyle's wide grin, so free of irony or calculation, stunned his godfather. Kyle embraced Hogan, his arms still tight as Hogan insisted again that he return home. Once alone, Hogan gazed listlessly about the townhome. There was only one place he could think to go.

"What the fuck was that?" the man demanded, glaring down at Hogan.

"I'm sorry, I must be—could you come back later?"

The man clubbed Hogan in the temple, his fist lifting to strike again. Hogan haltingly placed his palm over his ear, acclimated again to the insistent techno beats. He should keep apologizing, before the scene turned nasty, but the words refused to depart. He was done apologizing. There was nothing sorry about him. He'd told himself that countless times, but now he actually believed it. He felt light, the weight of shame falling from his frame.

"A college boy wouldn't try this shit," the man said. Hogan stared blankly ahead as the man softened. "Where's your stash?" he demanded.

"My what? My—?"

"Least you owe me for these fucking blue balls."

"I got tweaked at home. I don't—"

"Shithead faggot!" He shoved Hogan to the concrete floor, ransacked the gym bag where Hogan kept his clothes, lubricant, bottled water and other items needed for serial sex. The man was bigger, younger, more aggressive. *He simply wanted a stronger buzz*, Hogan told himself with a rush of relief. After scattering his things to the floor, the man batted Hogan's head with an open palm, glared at him cowering at his feet, shaking his head in disgust. Hogan closed his eyes. As the man left, he bitched about the sudden cold, promised the empty hallway he'd find the manager. Once Hogan opened them, he was alone, the door left wide open. A couple of twinks with shaven chests and twittering voices paused at the doorway.

"Hey, asshole," one said. "You're bleeding."

"You don't have AIDS, do you?" the other asked.

Without answering, without looking, Hogan swung shut the door. His head throbbed, especially his inner ear. The pain would worsen once the dope wore off. He leaned into the closed door. He swore to himself that there was no need to be sorry, but his instant of self-worth was already waning. As always, she appeared with no warning.

"Hogie," Mama said. "You can't let boys rough you up like that."

The bow tie, the sequins, the tap shoes.

"I'm fine, Mama."

She tenderly tilted his head this way and that. "Can you hear me good?" she shouted into his ear. He nodded, the tears starting to fall. He felt so thankful that at least one person *knew* him.

"I fucked up, Mama."

"That's all in the past."

"You were right. I can't make a good decision to save my life."

"Open the door, son."

"I can't, Mama. Those assholes are all outside."

She took his hand from his ear and held it between hers. "Open the door."


*Mama dances alone onstage. No music, just the mesmerizing rhythm of her steps against the stage. A harsh white spotlight washes the age from her face, gives it a hard sheen. A five-year-old boy sits in the front row amidst a sea of empty seats. Mama strikes her final pose and grins as if the whole auditorium were applauding, not just the boy.*

*She gestures for him to join her onstage. Without hesitation, he dashes up to the one person in his life who would always love him, never leave him. Mama picks up her son, and he melts into her arms' surprising strength. Despite the empty chairs, applause thunders around them. The spotlight grows more intense, but its light is warm and welcoming. Mama loves her Hogan—it is certain like the sunrise.*

# DIFFERENT DIRECTIONS

## JAMES ROWLAND

I don't think of the consequences as the door slams shut. It's just a reflex. Sometimes, something is annoying and you need to be rid of it: peeling wallpaper, a chewed up pillowcase or a scruffy looking human being. Eddie stands on my doorstep, his voice causing a ripple to run through the neighbours' curtains. The door sits between us. It's the easiest thing in the world to do. I take hold of the handle and swing it shut on Eddie's gaunt, reddening face. Within a second, his oblong head is hidden by an inch of wood. His messy blond hair is already slipping from my memory. Trying to remember exactly what shade of blue his eyes are, I stumble upon the difference between the ocean and the sky. Already a sensation floods through my veins. My heart screams at me to fling open the door and see his stupid face again.

The act of door slamming is an instinct, nothing but a cringe before a punch. It's a damning snap judgement on human nature. We would rather shut out alternate points of view rather than consider them. I don't want to hear why Eddie placed a week's wages on Snacks for Humans, or Daffodil Dundee, or whatever the horse's bloody name was. I just want to shut him up. The door acts as the perfectly honed instrument, a crafted skill sent down from generation to generation. I slam it like millions have before me. The reflection of humanity in the mirror isn't why I fall to the bottom step of the staircase, cradling my knees in arms. It isn't why I feel as if someone had reached inside me and squeezed my stomach. I feel sick because Eddie is quiet outside. His tight jeans and silly pop culture shirt are gone, cleansed from the front step like the non-believer from the church. Eddie is gone and I know why.

To be honest, I have no idea if my parents really loved each other. The only memories I have were of them loving me. The occasional glimpse of being swung around a flowering back garden by my father; a moment caught in my memory of paddling out to sea, safe in the protective cocoon of my mother's warm hand. I don't remember any closeness for each other. They never really seemed a team, more rival captains of two fading sides, leaders who had grown familiar with each other. They were France and Britain in a Cold War world: respect, mutual distrust, unimportant, but ultimately having a common goal. Me.

The façade was so passionless that whenever it broke, I used to sit at the wall and listen. People roll their eyes and ask what type of person watches soap operas. Humans do. Some just find their source closer to home. It was interesting; it was different. I learnt that whereas my mother grew frantic and angry, my father always stayed calm. He never yelled. As a child, I adored that. He seemed so in control. When I was older, I realised that his calmness wasn't an iron personality, but rather solid, steel indifference. My mother screamed through their fights because she cared.

Every so often, I would sit down and explain to my father what was wrong in the house. He never stopped me and explained I was too young to understand. I was treated like an adult and it was wonderful. Except, I wasn't an adult. I was seven. Through the course of any one day, I might have wanted to be a pirate, a nurse, a doctor, a detective and then a horse. With the benefit of later years, I wouldn't suggest that someone wishing to be a horse could offer much insight into relationship troubles. For some reason, my father did.

I told him how my mother had done things wrong, or why she needed to do this. Mummy never wants to do anything. She's always thinking of reasons why not to. I wanted to go to the model village, but she said it was going to rain and we would go

another day. The injustice of it all burned me. She was a closed door, refusing to budge as I ached to explore the world beyond the structurally unsound walls of my family. It wasn't fair.

But you, I'd rave to my father, always want to do new things. You wanted to see what the carnival was like. If there was a new ice cream flavour at our favourite shop, you'd be right there to try it. If I wanted to go and see a castle, you'd take me to one. You were always open, willing to let life live. He would nod and agree and I would feel very wise.

I never told my mother anything. She had my sister to be concerned with, who appeared without warning as if to somehow pave over the potholes in my parents' marriage. Being older, having experienced those golden years of an eldest child's reign, I wasn't very good at sharing. I had to share my mother; my father was all mine.

For years I thought I remembered perfectly the day my mother slammed the door on him. My father had spent the morning mowing the lawns; I watched Saturday morning cartoons. In the kitchen, my mother baked a cake. Years later, when I talked to her about it, she pointed out I was wrong. My memories of that entire week had converged on a single day, giving it length and flavour that was adopted from its neighbours. The day the door slammed was a Wednesday during the school holidays and they had both tidied their bedroom. It was when she found the letters. In the grand scheme of things, I suppose Eddie's horses probably rank somewhere below those letters. Most things do.

There had been yelling from upstairs, but I hadn't moved to listen. I was playing balloon football with my younger sister.

She seemed happy about being used as a springboard for a red ball of latex. At the time, I swore I heard the broken glass first and then a faint thud. I didn't know what that meant then and now I think the thud came first, the broken glass a retaliatory action. My sister looked curious and I had a strange feeling this was something she wasn't meant to hear. I could hear because I was allowed. After all, I was seven. But she was young and it was my job to distract her; I threw the balloon at her face and she giggled some more.

Somehow they ended up on the front step. It was new and foreign, something that had never happened before. The front step seemed to be a threshold. I had never seen them argue outside, not even in the back garden where everyone fought about flowers, lawns, and the accuracy of a backyard LBW decision. My sister began to cry, the balloon no longer bouncing off her face. For once, I went to the door not as a spectator but a vested party, wanting to make sure everything was okay. They never argued around me. Once, when it was a question of money, I walked into the arena and pretended I wanted breakfast. They immediately stopped whatever they were doing and didn't yell again for the next few days. For me, the arguments about money seemed the most important. I got one gold coin in pocket money a week, enough to buy two chocolate bars, though I never did. Instead, I kept them safe because it seemed like an incredibly rare event. With Eddie's voice still silent, I look at my shoes in front of me, old and faded, and suppose habits never change.

My father stood on the front step, much like Eddie did. Unlike Eddie, there was no neighbour-alerting yelling. If anything he seemed to regard the whole thing like slowing for a toll booth, boring but necessary. If only she'd listen to him, he began; there was a simple explanation for everything. My mother slammed the door shut. It seemed so calculated at the time. Now I understand better. You just need to make the voice stop.

When I was little, I used to sleep with my bedroom door open. It took several more years for me to have a television in my room. The box then served as a night light for the rest of my adolescence. Without that third parent, the glow from the hallway's light was needed to seep into my room. Having the door open was a necessity for another rational reason, though. I needed to be able to see the monsters. If the door was closed, who knew what was massing at the threshold, waiting to take me away. By the time I moved away from home, I always kept the entrance to my room shut. I didn't want to wake up to a set of eyes staring at me from the darkness. Children have a better understanding of doors than adults. When an adult closes a door, the problem is finished. It's not an issue until it's opened again. Children understand that when the door is closed, anything could happen behind it.

The door slammed shut on my father. I couldn't see what was happening to him. It was as if I'd been thrown into a deep swimming pool with no idea how to float. The cold water knocked the air right out of me. I ran back into the living room, ignoring how my toe jammed against the edge of the couch, and yanked back the curtains. The fabric fell from its hooks. I needed to see him there. If I saw my father there, standing on the front step, everything would be okay. Otherwise, he might be gone, he might walk down the garden path and I would never see him again.

He wasn't there. There was no one on the front step; no one walking down the garden path. The street was empty. Even with tears streaming down my face, the panic inside me had to share accommodation with curiosity. He couldn't have moved that quickly. I had only taken seconds to reach the window. Maybe he was still there, right at the door, somehow tucked out of view. I ran past my mother, ignoring her feeble pleading for the door to stay closed, and swung it open, ready to hold tightly to my father and to never let go. He wasn't there. I sobbed.

For the two days following my father's disappearance, my mother was remarkable. I only realised how incredible she had been a few years ago as we sipped wine together, celebrating my graduation from university. While friends came over, an Ancient Greek procession of women and food marching into the house, in reality, she was alone. Even now I can't understand how she managed to cope. Her husband had left and without him their home must have felt like an ill-fitting hand-me-down from an older sibling. She had a baby girl to worry about and her eldest child spent hours on the front step, closing the door and opening it again, trying to unlock some secret that perhaps only adults knew. The problem was grown-ups could rationalise in the face of the obviously unexplainable and I was still years away from reaching that double-sided nirvana.

Placed in front of my father's mysterious disappearance, my mother was as resolute as the door itself. He had obviously stormed off. But, I said, talking to her more than I'd done for years; I was at the window, I would have seen him. As she explained how I had

probably just missed him, I didn't notice the watering eyes or the colour draining from her face. It would have been the last thing she wanted to talk about, yet she did because she knew it was important for me to understand. I grew more frustrated, worrying more and more that she was right. The only recourse open to me was to stand at the front door, slamming it shut over and over again, wondering if anything would happen.

It took two days for my mother's patience to snap. She came storming out of the kitchen, soapy yellow gloves on her hands, and yelled at me to come inside. Inexplicably, something flashed in my mind. Everything made sense. It was my mother who closed the portal-like door, who slammed it shut on my father's face. I had been closing the door myself, not out of anger but despair. It wouldn't work the same way as it did when my father disappeared. The cogs in my brain began to turn. Maybe if she did the same to me, if she closed the door in anger at me, I would find out what happened. All I had to do was make her slam the door. It was child's logic at its finest.

I don't remember what I said to her. I think I forgot it intentionally. My mother doesn't remember the incident at all and so I'm too afraid to ask her, in case it triggers her memory and she suddenly feels what she felt when I screamed something terrible at her from the door. It was like I had taken a swing at her. She staggered back, reeling in a way I thought only people on television did. She didn't slam the door; she just stared. So I tried again. I can't remember what horrible thing I said, but I know I yelled it to her twice. It's enough to make my face still burn red hot. The second time, something snapped. She rushed forward and swung the door so fast I barely caught sight of the hallway disappearing from view in front of me.

Breathing deeply, sucking in a mouthful of air, it felt as if I was breathing yoghurt or a smoothie. The oxygen was thick in my mouth, lodging in my throat. It burned at my insides. My nostrils sniffed, smelling the dampness of clothes left to sit in a washing machine for too long. The air continued to grow outwards in my mouth. I tried to scream, my eyes watering, but it took too much effort for any sound to charge its way up my windpipe. Gulping quicker, filling my mouth with even more of the thick unyielding air, I noticed my front door had disappeared.

My heart stopped. My eyes grew wide as I spun on my feet. The sky was obsidian, a glinting blackness hovering high above me. Yet, the towering trees were easily visible for miles into the distance. There was a light, a glow as natural as if the sun still sat within the inkiness above. I was deep within some forest made tunnel, trees from one side of the path desperately reaching out to their brethren on the other. There was the trickle of running water, the sound twisting in an echo, my ears struggling to place its source. I turned to the left and saw a gentle river, wide and clear. Looking to the right, I spied the same river, a reflection of the one on my left. Somehow I knew that neither river existed at the same time. If I saw the one, the other was unmade. No matter how fast I spun, I couldn't prove the ridiculous idea. Standing there too stunned to cry, the thickness in my mouth slowly sank to my lungs. It tasted of soap.

A figure was standing far behind me. He was at one end of the tree tunnel, unmoving, silhouetted in that unnatural light. He lifted one hand, nothing more than a shadow, and beckoned me toward him. It didn't look like my father, yet I assumed this must have been the place he went to. The figure looked like a man, but one who was drawn too quickly and without attention to detail. His legs were uneven and arms seemed to grow out of his top ribs. I ran. Throughout our childhood, my sister always welcomed strangers: at weddings, birthdays, sporting events. I distrusted them. I never spoke to anyone who hadn't been introduced to me by someone I already knew. As adults, I'm the optimist; she's the pessimist.

Only one direction was open: running deeper into the tree tunnel. The mirror river circled around me. It blocked any chance at breaking free from the path. The figure followed. He walked, never quickening, never slowing. I was fast. I had beaten Adam Treadwell at Sports Day. The figure that never ran was faster. He grew larger every time I looked back at him. He never became anything more than a shadow. Over my shallow breathing, sucking in that thickened air like my favourite drink, I could hear something whisper in the air. It wasn't birdsong or even the ripples of the wind rustling through the leaves of the forest. Rather, it was a voice, gently singing, teasing my ears with sweet sounds and it felt familiar, a song that had followed me from my crib.

It crossed my mind that I couldn't keep running forever. My legs were getting sore and my insides burned from swallowing so much of the strange, soap flavoured air. The figure grew closer. I wondered if I should stop. Maybe just let him take me. He was going to catch me anyway. I was hurting myself for no reason. I pushed the thought from my mind. It seemed to me that I had only one choice: keep moving. Beyond the trees, there might be safety. There might be my father. The thought filled my lungs. I ran faster. The figure grew closer. The singing grew more insistent, snatched whispers of French gathering around me like a coat and I clung to them. They were a familiar presence in a strange place.

Ending like an accident-touched love, the tree tunnel vanished and I was running through a field, a tiny cottage sitting on the horizon. I hadn't heard of the word 'rustic' yet, but the cottage fitted the term perfectly. It was made of honest, hard stone and natural, thick wood. Round like an Anglo-Saxon house, a chimney sat haphazardly on top, balancing like some neglectful god had dropped it from high above. There was a great oak door and I ran to it, yanking it open as the figure emerged from the tree tunnel behind me. Forgetting that this wasn't my house, ignoring the strange black sky that shone like the sun and the gentle music that whispered as the wind, I slammed the door shut and pulled the great wooden lock into place.

Breathing heavily, I braced myself against the door. The heave would come at any second. With far greater strength than my own, the figure would push at the entrance and snatch me. My lungs filled with air. I was desperately trying to stay afloat in the black sea of my fear. The assault never came. Allowing my hand to slip from the old oak door, I glanced out of a nearby window and saw the figure loitering at the edge of the forest. He seemed unable to cross the threshold and I wondered if he was some sort of fairy spirit. My bedtime stories were once filled with such things.

The cottage I had flung myself into was devoid of life. It made me feel better. An empty house has always been my preferred state. At ten, it meant indoor cricket and loud music. At twenty, the emptiness was freedom from worrying about creaking bed springs. At thirty, it just means quiet, which is the greatest commodity of all. In that cottage, the emptiness meant life. The air was lighter inside, easier to swallow. The strange natural light filled the single room comfortably. There was a fireplace, but it looked like my grandfather's cricket bat, cracked from years of neglect. Somehow nestled in the corner of a round room, there was a bed and across from it a small kitchen. I felt my stomach growl.

The windows scattered conservatively around the room were small and round. They were like portholes and I felt as if I was in a small sailing ship, a tiny cabin offering safe passage from a fierce storm. The windows were all open and as I went to each they stubbornly refused to close. I pushed and banged, but they stayed ajar, the hinges having long since lost their final battle with rust. I left them open. The figure between the trees, still nothing but a darkened shadow, couldn't climb through them. With the ancient door acting like a castle between me and the strange world, my heartbeat grew slower and my breathing steadied. My stomach continued to growl. I softly padded over the grassy floor, looking all around for a pair of eyes to catch me where I shouldn't be. There was no one. I think I decided then that the house must have been foreclosed, like the homes on either side of my own. Foreclosure wasn't something I completely understood, but I saw it as houses falling down the cracks, where nobody owned anything. Houses like the ocean.

Because I was hungry and I was young, it seemed perfectly acceptable for me to raid the pantry for any leftover food. I opened the door and gave a little squeak. The cupboard was like an undiscovered Wonder of the World. There was roast chicken and the smell of honey-coated pork. Pots of steaming vegetables waited patiently next to spices and condiments I had never seen before. There were eggs and fresh milk, lettuces, and all kind of things that looked savoury but smelt like desserts. I stared at it all, mouth open and saliva dribbling down my lips. When I went to reach for the food, though, I suddenly felt my stomach tighten. I didn't know how to prepare any of these wonderful ingredients. I wasn't sure what went best with pork and what shouldn't be put alongside salmon. I panicked, worrying that I may confuse the spices or burn the eggs. It seemed like I could have made any meal I wanted, ate anything at all, but with that pantry in front of me, I froze. I took a slice of homemade bread, the smell filling my nose, and buttered it with the softest butter I'd ever seen, and sat down on the bed to eat. I still regret that choice even now.

Only once a liberal scattering of crumbs were sown across my lap did I notice the air growing thicker again. It was harder to swallow. Expanding, it pressed my throat open like a balloon threatening to pop. I gulped over and over, trying to find the thin air. I looked at the open windows. They were the threat. I attacked them once more, pushing, banging, slamming and still they refused to close. I screamed. I begged them to shut. They did nothing, leaving me at the mercy of the rigid air.

The figure was gone from the forest. Checking every window, not catching sight of the shadow stalking me, I rushed over to the door, ready to make a break to safety. I had no idea where safety was. Yet, as my hands fumbled with the lock, the wood growing damp with sweat, the door remained stubbornly closed. Tears streamed down my face. I kicked at the wood, but it still refused to budge.

Looking back at the windows, I swallowed back my tears. They were small but so was I. Running back and forth across the cottage, I drank the thick air, stacking firewood under one of the porthole openings. Managing to stick my head through the window, I saw something shift just out of view. I turned. My shoulders dug into the hinges. The figure stood a metre away. My heart dropped through my stomach. He didn't have a face but I knew he was smiling, smiling in the way adults did when they had tricked you in some way. Jumping back, trying to escape his outstretched hand, my head banged against the window so hard everything went black. It's a silly thought, but I don't think I fell unconscious. Rather, I was floating in the obsidian sky, looking in every direction, only seeing more darkness spreading out in front of me until my eyes opened and I was huddled by the oak door. It was a comforting presence. It remained resolutely closed. It had protected me. My head throbbed and I reached back, rubbing the large bump under my hair.

I stayed away from the windows after that, wishing they would shut even for an hour. I took the bedding and made a fort under the watch of the door. Occasionally, I'd get up to butter another slice of bread. The natural light which had to be artificial did not go away and I struggled to sleep. Eventually I rolled myself into a cocoon, the scratchy fabric dulling the sounds of the figure pacing around the cottage. I think if I was there now, I never would have slept. I would have spent night after night wondering where I was, what the figure was, how I got there, and whose house I was in. But seven-year-old me didn't think about those things. All I thought about then was that it felt late and I had run so very far, and I was tired. In the darkness of the bedding, I slept.

Sometimes, I wake up and feel as if I have only fallen asleep minutes ago, though the clock tells me differently. This was the opposite. My mother swore I was only gone a few hours and yet I think I must have slept for weeks. A single dream stretched on and on without end. I sat behind a desk, never moving, always sitting, and people would enter the empty room and talk to me. I knew some of them. My mother came and then my father, both to let me know that they loved me and my heart doubled in size. My father asked me to stay with him; my mother didn't. At times, my visitors were unexpected. My music teacher walked in and began a long monologue about my tastes in television. The person that caught my attention most was the elderly woman, someone I still don't recognise, who took my hand in hers and gently stroked it, running her nails across my palm. She nodded and told me that not all distractions are bad. With a smile, she told me sometimes you should allow yourself to leave the path you had set. I can still smell the mint on her breath.

When I opened my eyes, I was surprised at how blue the sky looked. It took me several moments to realise that blue was its natural colour and not obsidian that glistens and shines as bright as the sun. I was standing in my front garden, several steps away from the path, the short grass gently massaging my toes in the breeze. Spinning around, I looked everywhere for the figure with no face. I searched for a shadow in the bushes. I waited for a figure in the distance. There was nothing but cars, real estate signs, and Mrs Treadwell pottering around her garden, nursing the hydrangeas. Tears in my eyes, I laughed and ran forward, flinging open the front door and rushing to the dining room, following the familiar sound of my mother's voice.

She screamed when she saw me and wrapped me in her arms, refusing to budge even after I said she was squeezing too tight. Her jumper scratched at my chin. Even though I had only been gone for a couple of hours, our dining room was filled with family, friends and two police officers who rolled their eyes, pocketed their notebooks and left after exchanging several words with my aunt. My mother kept hugging me as people asked where I went. No one believed me. I told the story over and over again, explaining that I think I found where my father was, and noticed several faces darken. I knew I had said something wrong, but I wasn't old enough to understand the implication. I tacked in the wind and lied, saying I had gone to the park and came up with the story. I wanted to trick people. What seemed ridiculous was now considered a very good tale, and people said perhaps if I did well in English, I could be a writer one day. I nodded, and thought of everything, or what a child considers everything, and asked if I could sleep. I never told anyone about the place again.

Two weeks later, my father returned. He had large, black bags under his eyes and looked as if he hadn't slept for the entire time he was gone. I knew then he had been to the same place as me, but I no longer wanted to talk about it. He hugged me, and I hugged him very tightly back, but then when he went to watch television, I went to the kitchen instead and helped my mother with dinner. When he moved out two months later, it wasn't a surprise to them when I said I wanted to stay with my mother. I was confused because it was a shock to me; I didn't know exactly why I made that choice till years later. It was something to do with the strange house in the stranger world. I knew, on some primal level, I was safer with my mother, the closed door and not the open window. She tried hard not to smile at the news and my father did his best not to look disappointed. He hugged me again and told me he wasn't angry, which I needed to hear more than anything in the world. He said he would come and visit. Sometimes he did.

I look down at my watch and it's been several hours since I slammed the door shut on Eddie's face. It only felt like minutes ago. Standing up, a prickling sensation shooting down my legs, I walk to the door and open it. He's gone. Of course, he is. It has been hours and he wouldn't stand on my front step forever. No doubt he's at the pub, drowning his sorrows. That's what I tell myself.

I wonder how long it will take for him to come back.

# DOG TRACK

## JAY CASELBERG

We knew about the route, knew about the stories that had always come from that particular track of road. That knowledge came early. The road ran between dense trees draped with moss, and moist with the dampness of despair. Shadows clustered between those ancient trunks, punctuated by bark faces, writhing in remembered misery. Though we called it 'road,' it was mere lip service to the concept. Little more than a rutted dirt track, runnels carving its surface, where the melt-water had cascaded along the packed red earth and stone, leaves and small branches lay in scattered piles along its edges. There were times when the local residents, the older members, their faces lined with parchment memories, would look to the gap between the trees where it disappeared into murky darkness and murmur amongst themselves. More than once, I'd heard the word 'release,' but it was nothing I would be seeking, no matter how sweet they might imagine it and despite their apparent longing. Whether it was touched by wisdom or something else, I didn't know. Personally, I felt there was an indescribable bravery within those words. For certain, our own time would come one day, but it wouldn't be yet. Even now, I cannot believe that Sonia deserved that particular version of what they called release.

We hadn't been residents of the tiny community long. After the whole company meltdown thing and the shit-storm that followed, Sonia and I had decided to take the money and run, build a new life for ourselves somewhere out of the hustle and bustle and escape the constant threats of retribution and the continuing reminders of the lives that had been destroyed along the way. Back to nature, or that was the dream. I'd never really pictured myself as a survivalist, one of those who live up in the hills with a weapons cache and stacked supplies should the Apocalypse come to pass. I guess Green Falls was somewhere in between. It had its fair share of eccentricities, and bit by bit we were learning the entrenched behaviours of those who had been here far longer than we had. Whether they were societal drop-outs or merely those come to seek an altruistic better life among the arbours, they were all here for their own reasons, just as we were. This tiny town was not exactly "off the grid," but it was as near as you might get to it and that suited us just fine. There were rumours of a pack of dogs in the surrounding hills, and whether you gave them credence or not, perhaps they too had their own reasons for being here, or so the stories went.

"Are you sure this is what you want, Jeff?" Sonia had asked, her hand gently cupped against my cheek on the night that we decided. I had looked into her eyes and known right then that it was.

"Hell, yes," I'd said. "*Hell*, yes."

We'd had reporters around again that morning. The whole damned thing just refused to go away.

I'd looked around our apartment, decked out in the comfortable yet functional, and realised that there was nothing there that I was really going to miss. In the end, it took us about three months to settle on Green Falls, but once we'd decided, that was that. Boxes, and movers and trading the car for a more utilitarian pickup and then we were there. As simple as that. We only had ourselves; no pets, no kids, but maybe that would change in our newly chosen home. Maybe we'd finally have that chance now. Some of the stuff we put into storage until we could work out what we really needed. There was no rush, after all. We had enough to survive on until I could pick up some consulting work on the side to stretch out the funds. Green Falls was remote, sure, but it was still within a sensible striking distance from the city. I had no desire to be forced into commuting if I had to, but at

least there was still that option. An hour and a half's driving distance was at the edge of acceptability and I had known people who'd had worse.

When we first actually arrived in town, if it could really be called a town rather than a loose collection of buildings that just happened to be in the same general vicinity, we noted the suspicious glances tracking us as we passed, or the outright hands-on-hips staring as we trundled along what passed for the main road. Welcome, it was not, but it was understandable. The good people of Green Falls liked their privacy, and they had no reason to open their arms to untested interlopers. Rather than being intimidated, we were reassured. It was an extra shield against everything we were hoping to escape. Somehow, some way, however, there always has to be an accounting; we just didn't know it then.

Our new house welcomed us with cobwebs and faint trails of dust, dirt and dried up leaf matter across the floors, and a taste of empty expectation. I hadn't asked about the previous owner, but he had been long gone from the little I'd been told. There was a large tank out the back, our water supply, and a generator just in case. To one side lay a stack of old firewood. I promised myself that if I was going to go rooting around in all that, I'd be sure to wear gloves. It didn't look like it had been touched for years. We'd need it; that was for certain. Winter darkness under shadowed trees and the chill that went with it meant the fireplace in the living room would get good use. I made a mental note to check the chimney. You never know what might have made itself comfortable inside and the last thing we wanted was a living room filled with smoke after building our first fire on a wet and chilly night. We spent a few minutes in the living room's centre, just breathing in the atmosphere, the scents of earth and old wood, standing side by side, our arms around each other, awash with the scent of not only dried leaves but also something else we couldn't quite pin down. Perhaps it was just the smell of age.

"Well, this is it," said Sonia as we slowly looked around, hardly believing that we were finally there. "Welcome to our new life."

She reached up and kissed me and then, ever practical, headed off to check out the rudely equipped kitchen. I spent some time locating a broom and then set about sweeping away some of the trails from the living room floor. By the time we'd finished humping boxes from the truck, we were exhausted and ended up collapsing together on the couch, not even bothering to remove the greying dust cover that lay draped across it. For now, we were just content to be there in each other's company among the boxes— no internet, no television and no one to call us, dust streaks marking our faces, badges of our labours. I stroked the back of Sonia's hair and felt months of tension fading away. We had actually finally done it.

Over the next couple of days, as we busied ourselves trying to get the place in some sort of order, we had a trickle of visitors, locals come to check us out, or genuinely there to welcome us. A hint of strangeness accompanied each of these visits, but I couldn't quite put my finger on it. Maybe it was just the nature of an isolated community.

"A word to the wise—watch the track, especially after dark." That came from Rose, one of the older visitors. We were standing out on the front porch, looking out at the trees when she said this. She tapped one extended finger against the side of her nose as she said it.

I frowned and shook my head. "What track is that?"

"See that little road over there? You can just see the start of it over there between the trees."

It wasn't much of a road, but I could see the place she indicated.

"So what is it I have to watch?" I asked.

She shook her head, licked her lips and then looked away, a troubled expression on her face. "Just take care," she said.

When I tried to press her further, she suddenly seemed to have forgotten to do something and hobbled back up the road glancing off into the trees as she went. Just once, she glanced back over her shoulder at us still standing out there on the porch, and turned away again with a little shake of her head.

"Well, that was odd," said Sonia, reaching for my hand.

"Wasn't it?" I said. "So what next?"

"The last of the boxes, I suppose."

And that was that.

That night, we heard the distant howling. I couldn't remember who had told us about the dog pack. There was something strange about the sound as we lay there in the darkness. It swelled and then suddenly cut out, then faded back in, interrupted. Outside, there was a slight wind—we could hear it stirring the branches—and I guessed that's what distorted the sound. Sonia reached for my hand under the covers as the mournful cries swelled in the outside blackness, filtering through the trees. Eventually, it faded altogether, and Sonia pulled herself closer to me, curling up against my body.

"God," she whispered into my shoulder. "I hope we don't get that every night." She gave a little shudder and pressed tighter against me, sliding her arm across me to lie across my chest. I repositioned myself to hold her close.

Eventually her breathing slowed again, became more regular, leaving me staring upwards, my eyes wide open watching the moving patterns of tree branches painted in shadows on the ceiling and listening to the intermittent rattle of the wind pushing against the glass. Eventually, I slept, despite the vague sense of unease working somewhere deep within the bottom of my stomach. In the distance, every now and again came that cry of the animals moving somewhere through the darkness.

There was no store, as such, anywhere within Green Falls, and we were forced into doing supply runs to the nearby, larger town of Layton's Crossing. On the way in, we both wondered who Layton was and what exactly he'd crossed. Whatever it was, it was lost somewhere in the shadows of history. Houses clustered on either side of something that was at least recognisable as a main street. The general store there was not much, but it was sufficient to keep us stocked for a few days, and I made a note that we'd have to think about heading further afield to do a bulk shop. Now with the pickup, we were in a position to do so. I also made a note that we should probably purchase a large freezer to keep us going—one of the things we'd never thought about that came with living off in the sticks. Sure, there was the generator and the water tank, but there were other things that those used to city life just didn't consider as we were starting to learn.

We were so busy getting the place in order, that it was several days before I took my first foray out into the surrounding trees. Sonia waved me off, still determined to concentrate on getting the cottage into a state that matched her particular expectations and that was fine. That vague sense of unease that had come on our first night in the new place had not gone away; it just lingered in the background, nothing expressly conscious, but there nonetheless. I was content just to wander out on my own, exploring. By the time I got back, Sonia might be ready to broach the boxes of books and start filling the empty shelves that stared at us accusingly from the living room walls. God knows, we needed something to fill the empty spaces that came with where we now lived. Where had people been before the advent of television and radio and the online presence? We'd never been much for Facebook and the like. It simply left is too vulnerable. Granted, it wasn't that primitive, and we hadn't yet thought about the practicality of exploring the options. We'd noticed a couple of tall dishes set high upon poles above the houses, but whoever had lived here before us in our little residence simply hadn't bothered. Perhaps I could ask Rose. As I headed out from our front steps, I made a mental note to speak to her another time, just on the off chance.

Heading out into the trees, it became clear fairly quickly exactly how isolated we really were, how far removed the little town of Green Falls really was. Within a couple of short minutes, I was swallowed up, dappled sunlight painting leaf litter with golden patches between the darker browns. The trees were old, I could see that, but there was new growth and smaller shrubby plants between. Something rustled through the ground cover, startled by the crunch of my step through old fallen bark and twigs.

I stopped for a few moments and listened. Somewhere off among the treetops, a bird belled its call, but it drifted vaguely through the air, its location impossible to determine. Patches of orange-brown earth painted with lighter humps of exposed stone peered through the brown cover of leaves as if the underlying bedrock was flexing its back, trying to break through the surface. The air was full of the scent of old leaves and even older wood, the taste of dampness creeping through. Of the town, I could hear nothing, no sign that there was any other human presence anywhere nearby, no planes, no grumbling traffic noise, nothing. A breeze stirred above through the branches, the foliage whispering all around me, and then it was gone. I closed my eyes and stood simply listening for a few moments, drinking in the unfamiliar sensation of solitude. Away in the distance, a crow's harsh voice interrupted the sound of creaking branches, and then all was silent once more. Here was I in the middle of nowhere, Sonia back at home, probably wiping sweat from her brow with the back of one hand, her hair tied back in a scarf, working hard, and I'd simply escaped. I let out a deep breath and continued walking.

A few minutes later, the trees gave way to a narrow strip running down the hill from the direction of town. It was rutted and worn, old stones and channels where the surface had eroded. It was barely a road— more like a firebreak between the trees. I stood at its edge, looking first one way, then the other. It seemed pretty innocuous. Why exactly had Rose warned us about it? I turned in the direction that led away from Green Falls, walking down the gentle slope. A breeze stirred the leaves all around me, but of birdsong, there was none. I'd not gone more than a hundred metres when I noticed a cluster of something further down, sitting in the middle of the trail. Bunched, white and brown, at first I thought it was a pile of old branches that had fallen from the surrounding trees, but as I got closer, the shapes resolved themselves into something else, something completely else. It was a pile of bones, white, yellow, darker brown strips still adhering to them. I stopped a few paces from them and looked up and down the trail. A little way off, there was something else, something lying scattered on the road's surface, something that could also be old discarded pieces of wood, but also maybe something else. I swallowed, suddenly feeling chill. The wind chose that moment to pick up a little. The groan of creaking wood stirred all around me. I crouched next to the scattered pile. They were definitely bones. I reached out with one finger to poke at them, then thought better of it and swallowing, rose to my feet. Far away, somewhere off through the trees, there was a howl, joined shortly after by another. Just then, I decided I didn't want to be there and I stepped off the rough road and back into the trees. The dog pack was somewhere out there. Sometimes a dog's howling is described as mournful; there was nothing mournful about that cry at all.

As I retraced my trail, back to the house, glancing nervously over my shoulder and starting at every unusual sound filtering through the trees, I decided that there had to be a logical explanation. A cow or something, probably. Likely it had wandered down the trail to die, the dog pack had found it and then…. That had to be it, although I wasn't so sure. The bones had not looked quite right, not like the bones of a cow. Perhaps it was some other wild creature. But that still didn't explain the similar pile that I'd seen further down the road.

Over the next couple of weeks, other things started to emerge about Green Falls, about our strange little chosen escape from the world. It was only later that things clicked together and I started to understand properly—random, seemingly unconnected things like the fact that Green Falls didn't seem to have anything resembling a cemetery. In my experience, even the smallest villages seem to have a small plot, an isolated field somewhere, where at least one person is laid to rest. There certainly wasn't a place of worship.

I went for several random wanders through the small cluster of houses and the surrounding trees, bumped into a few of the local residents here and there, once or twice stopped for polite conversation, although there was something guarded about the way they looked at me, how their eyes lingered on Sonia when she accompanied me. Rudy Jeffers was one such. He was out the front of his house when we wandered up, that particular day. He straightened as we approached, pushing lank grey tresses out of his face and peering at us curiously with bleary eyes.

"You're the new folk, aren't you?" His gaze stayed on Sonia as he spoke, and then he reluctantly dragged his attention back to me.

"That would be us," I responded. "Jeff and Sonia Martin."

"Rudy Jeffers," he said. "You people are in the old Logan place, right?" He'd made no move to approach, to shake hands, move anywhere outside the boundary of his own property. He shook his head, his gaze drifting away from us. "Yeah, Tommy Logan. That one went early."

"How do you mean?" I asked him.

He tilted his head a little, looking up at the treetops—anywhere but directly at us.

"We all go, eventually. That one just chose to go early." Again, he shook his head.

There was something strange about the way he said it. He rubbed fingers across his forehead and then his attention wandered further down the road to the start of that almost path leading off between the trees.

"Sometimes," he said, "I guess it just gets too hard." He frowned and scrunched up his face, and then shook himself.

"Well, try to enjoy it for as long as you are here," he said. "However long that might be. As long as you can, anyway."

"Thanks…" I said, uncertainly, intending to follow up with something polite but I was already talking to his retreating back. We watched him shuffle across the front yard, up the steps and into his house, closing the door behind him.

I looked at Sonia and she looked at me. "What was that?" she said.

"I have no idea."

The longer we spent in Green Falls, the stranger things were. Something he'd said though gave me an uneasy feeling. Something had happened to the previous resident of our place, Tommy Logan. The people who'd sold it to us had been fairly quiet about that. The way Rudy Jeffers had spoken about it made me think it was nothing good. I took Sonia's hand and drew her way. We weren't going to gain anything just standing there.

A couple of days later, I bumped into Rose. To date, she had still been the most forthcoming of the locals. Everyone else pretty much kept to themselves, with little more than a nod, or that strange lingering gaze before they turned away again.

"Hi, Rose. Glad I ran into you. I just

had a quick question for you, if you don't mind. I thought maybe you'd know."

"Hmmm?" she said vaguely.

"What is the Tommy Logan story?"

The vagueness left her face immediately and she narrowed her eyes, peering up into my face. Around us, a gentle breeze stirred the leaves. One or two spiralled down to the ground beside us, dry and brown.

"Who have you been talking to?"

I rubbed the back of my neck. "It was just something Rudy Jeffers, I think that's his name, told us. Maybe it's nothing. Maybe I just misheard."

She was silent for several moments.

"We didn't expect it so soon, with Tommy," she said and looked away. "Have the dreams started yet?" she said, without meeting my eyes.

"Dreams? What dreams?"

This time she did look directly into my face. "You will know what dreams when they come or you wouldn't have to ask."

"So tell me."

She shook her head. "No, I don't want to talk about that," she said, turning completely away from me and starting to head back up the main street. "None of us want to talk about that, despite the sins we might carry with us."

"Rose?"

She lifted a hand, waving my query away without turning, shaking her head, leaving me standing there in the middle of the street, my mouth open in disbelief.

"Rose?" I called after her again, but there was no further response.

When I got back home and discussed the incident with Sonia, she looked troubled.

"This is just getting weirder and weirder. I'm not sure.... " She gave a sigh. "Maybe we should just pack up and leave."

"What? We can't do that."

"Why? Why not?" Her hands were on her hips now. "There's nothing holding us here. We're not comfortable. That much is clear."

"What? We've barely been here long enough to get a proper feel for the place. Despite everything, I think this is right. We both agreed. Do you really want to go back to all that crap we left behind?"

She turned away from me then, letting out an exasperated breath, and then steadied herself.

"You're right," she said. "Of course you're right. It's just...." She turned back to face me again. "You said Rose said something about dreams."

"Yes. But she wouldn't tell me anything else."

Sonia bit her lip, closed her eyes, and then opened them again. "It's just that for the last couple of nights..."

"What?"

"Well I've been having this recurring... no, forget it."

"Sonia, tell me."

"No, forget it. It's nothing. I don't want to talk about it."

What had Rose said?

*None of us want to talk about that.*

That night I had my first one.

I was lying in amongst the trees, flat on the ground. Dry leaves pressed into my face. Small twigs crunched under me as I shifted, and I felt a sense of panic. I had to stay still. No noise, no noise at all. I bit my lip and held my breath, willing myself to quiet. Indistinct sounds drifted through the trees. Somewhere, not too far off, came animal cries, no, not just animals, dogs...that's what they were, dogs. The moon was bright, its pearl light beaming down in patches through the branches. And there was a smell, something, feral? No, it was something other, with the hint of decay.

Between the tree trunks, I could see a patch of road, or at least something that aspired to be a road. It looked familiar, as if I'd been there before. Then I realised; I had been there before. There, in front of me lay a pile of bones, no, more a cluster, their detail standing out clearly in the moonlight. Oh, God, I was there. My heart flipped and I drew in a sharp breath with the realisation. Noises drifted through the trees, through the air above me. Something screeched. A bird? Or....

I knew I had to lie still. I couldn't move. If I moved, they would see me. I strained, concentrating my vision on that cluster of bones. No, I had been right. It wasn't a cluster, it was more defined than that, and it was bound in something—thin rope or fraying string. It was more than bones. Scraps of something adhered to the smooth curves, and the shape was familiar. Not just bones. It was a ribcage. Bound there, lying in the road's centre, it was a ribcage. A snuffling sound came from the shadows around me, and then I could see them. It was the dog pack, loping down the trail, five or six of them. They paused to sample the air, heads lifted, then one bent to sniff at the bones. It was close, close to me, nearer than the others who were standing, scanning through the trees, their heads swinging slowly. Something was wrong with the head of the one closest to me. I peered at it, desperate not to move, but I had to know. One complete side of the animal's jaw looked like it had been eaten away, receding, exposing yellowing teeth down one side. Raw flesh ran in a thin band around the edges. I swallowed, my heart beating faster.

As if noticing my scrutiny, the animal lifted its head, turning its gaze towards the trees where I lay.

Deep within its eyes something glowed, and that fleshless side grinned at me. In that instant, the beast lifted its head and howled. One by one, its companions turned their faces to the moon and joined the cry, barking, howling.

The one closest to me turned its face back towards me and started to growl, lips drawing back from its teeth on the side that still had flesh and skin and fur.

I woke, my heart pounding, the sweat slick across my forehead and chest. I sat up in bed, staring at the darkness at the blankness of the wall in front of me.

I must have cried out, because Sonia reached for me, her hand resting on my arm

"It was the dream wasn't it?" she said.

I turned to look at her shadowed face. Moonlight came through the window, painting it with pale light.

"It was the dream," she said again.

"What dre—" I started to say, but then I saw the knowledge in her eyes.

Just at that moment, off in the darkness, out amongst the trees, the dogs began to howl.

The dreams have not gone away. Always they are the same. Every couple of nights they are back, either Sonia, or me, or both of us together and we sit holding each other in our shadowed room, the sound of dogs in the darkness. We wonder if it was Green Falls that drew us to it, but that was six months ago now. We tried to leave, once or twice, but there's something here that holds us. It's us if the will just trickles out of us, defying our attempts. Now, the local Green Falls residents look at us differently. Something has changed. Somehow they

know, and we share our lingering looks,
filled with the knowledge of what's out there.
Maybe it's different, because now, truly,
we've become Green Falls residents too.

Our time will come. I know it will.
One of these days, all of the regret and
accumulated guilt will catch up with us.
There will always be retribution. It's just
how long it takes. Perhaps we'll take the
walk down that road together; perhaps we
won't. I am still not convinced that Sonia
deserves this despite being complicit in some
of the things that went on and her support
throughout. Is complicity enough?

Regardless, the track is still there. It's
not going away. I can feel it now.

The pack is there. It's waiting for us.

I can feel its patience.

# HEART OF THE MOON

## JENNIFER BENNINGFIELD

### MONDAY

I'm a young man by pretty much any standard. My mind, my body, young. Old ways of treatment will benefit from the augmentation of fresher methods, and I'm very grateful to you for realizing this. Because of your willingness, your open-mindedness, as well as the fact that this will all be *entre nous*...I shall aim to be as honest and forthright in this journal as I am able.

I can turn the sun silver. I have done so. Only...no one else has ever seen it! Only me. Me, "the boy with the topaz eyes." That's what my grandmother used to call me, in the days when she had cause to call.

I can see the wind on occasion. I can see it now, in fact, buffeting the painted brick of this apartment building. The wind looks like a grey-white wave of water. (You must've been wondering.) It leaves nothing behind in its wake, at least not that I can detect from an admittedly limited vantage point.

Have you ever read *Matilda*? Or at least know the basic plot through cultural osmosis? Little girl accidentally discovers that she possesses telekinetic powers when the headmistress at school sends her over the edge. She's stunned—and thrilled. She realizes that she can harness the force within, use it to fight back against the negative forces in her life. So she practices moving objects. She also feels an intense heat in her eyes as she does so. I have tried—and tried—but I am seemingly at the mercy of these peculiar hallucinations. Which, incidentally, provide me with no extra sensation whatsoever.

Have you ever walked down a hallway that narrows with every step forward? Have you ever opened a refrigerator and all you saw was a white and yellow light so bright you had to throw your hands over your eyes to keep from going blind?

Objects are one thing, but the people around me also tend to undergo these peculiar transformations. I've told you some vague examples. Their arms stretch to the consistency of pulled taffy, skin flapping wretchedly. Their heads alter shape, their eyes and ears blink in and out of my sight. Try having a conversation—try exchanging mere pleasantries—with a person who no longer fits the established criteria of "person." Like, Joan Miro would be weirded out by the stuff I see sometimes.

Most of my friends don't know. The few I have told had reactions other than sympathetic and sensitive. This distresses me less and less more and more. I am not so young that I do not realize most of the people on the planet do not care about anything they cannot actually *see* or *touch*.

I have a saying: never judge a day by its cloud cover. Disasters can, have and will go down on lovely mornings. If someone walks outside and instantly looks up to the sky for some indication or guidance or whatever, they're already way off and should probably head back inside and bury themselves under every blanket they own.

The shoe store I work at is one of six in the state. Scuttlebutt is that by the end of next year, another six will be up and running. I heartily look forward to working at zero of them by the end of next year. Sure, we sell relatively high-end footwear with the emphasis on comfort, but I'm still a salesman at day's end. If it weren't for the weekly customer who comes in, walks around and around until finally approaching one of us to utter some variant of the question, "Where are your Jordans?", I'd have quit already. Oh my God, the ones who get agitated when told we don't sell overpriced basketball shoes are the best. I imagine they mutter about us the rest of the day!

I'm amazed, day in and day out, at the people I see who are so picky about what they put on their feet when they so *clearly* have a carefree attitude about what goes over the rest of their body. "Slept In This" is the de rigueur style for most men around here aged 16-39 and the women? The gaucheries abound.

This place might not be Paris, but I still make the effort to look nice. My clothes *fit*. No sagging permitted. Chuck Taylors for casual evenings and Hugo Boss Italian leather cap toe Oxfords for fancier ones. (I love leather; the compliment you paid my jacket at the start of our very first session was just one of many I received that week.)

I'd like to reiterate here…I am most interested in the "how" of my condition. The "why," frequently the biggest puzzler, is actually not in this case. I believe I've sussed out the reason, please hear me out. From quite young, I realized that my surroundings were insufficient for my imagination. I've never been especially creative, so I never wrote or drew or recorded anything based on what went on inside my head, I just thought and pondered and daydreamed and pored over images on TV and inside magazines. Bright, glamorous…somewhere else!

Then came the day. The boom, the bloom.

When Matilda received her redemption—when she was placed properly in her school, when her home life went from catastrophic to compassionate—she lost her powers. When I finally save up enough to move from here to a city with actual culture—it doesn't have to be Paris, at least not right away—I suspect these funny visions will not make the trip with me.

### TUESDAY

One day last April I saw exclusively in red, white and blue. Definitely the most patriotic day of my life so far. I was downright *jubilant*!

When I returned home, I showered (in Smurf blood) and made the unorthodox decision to fix a pancake dinner. Three pancakes, to be precise, and wouldn't you know—each was a different color! One red, one white, one blue. The sight awed me so that I eschewed butter and syrup. I wanted those glorious circles of starch to remain unblemished as I devoured them.

My vision returned to standard by bedtime, but that was fine by me. Felt post-coital, honestly.

Or at least I think so. Honestly it's been a few months since my last time. I'm casual about sex, but I'm not stupid. It's safety first, always. I've had six partners in total, all but one of them other men. And the one girl? She was my first time. It's not as though the experience was so underwhelming that I decided to try "the other side," I've always been curious. Some might say that qualifies me as a "bisexual," but I don't really think so. And what *I think* is *what matters*.

Today I chatted with Drew during lunch break. I haven't told you the circumstances of our first meeting, have I? Across a crowded room, our eyes locked, the magic happened. Although in reality, none of that. We met in line at the Orange Julius at the shopping center. Now that I'm thinking back, one could say we met in the middle, since the OJ itself is located in the center of the center. Oh that's funny. I should mention that to him next time, but I probably shouldn't. I'm certain he realized that long

ago, maybe even during that first meeting, and he would think a bit less of me if I let slip that it took me months.

We see each other two times a week, maybe three. There's no planning ahead, and sometimes I don't feel like a mango smoothie. Sometimes I don't even leave the store for lunch. But today we grabbed our drinks and then a table out in front of the OJ. His job at Anne Taylor's doesn't provide him with much in the way of ridicule-worthy customers, so as usual it was up to me to amuse him with stories of mismatched sock-wearing, soiled diaper-smelling mouth-breathers who expect every shoe store to be like Payless.

Drew doesn't need to even speak. I'm more than happy to blah blah, just to sit across from him and take in the sight of those caramel-colored curls that make my teeth ache. (His are perfect, incidentally.) He's loose with his limbs, but tight with his words. The simplest motions he makes just dazzle me. (And I once saw a cat's head and tail switch positions!) He lives, unfrazzled. I know he'll be an enormous influence on my life, I just haven't figured out how yet.

I don't hate selling shoes for an alleged living, but I don't love it either. In addition to the laughably self-important floor manager, I work alongside one other person, a woman in her thirties with six siblings and a sibilance that makes my jaw clench. Fortunately, she doesn't speak much. Only when the demands of the job call out.

Walking home from the bus station, I took a detour to Barson Park, which is called "Barkson" by lots of locals thanks to its popularity with dog owners. I'm not one of those dreadful people who prefer domestic animals to other human beings, but I definitely prefer dogs over children. If the weather's pleasant enough, the kids will be out in abundance, but usually the four-legged responsibilities outnumber the two-legged ones at the Park.

On either side of the bell tower that juts up from the center of the park like, "Bitch, fuck you, I'm a bell tower," are two walking paths. I always follow the left one, which affords me a view of the lake. I never dawdle, just move long enough and strong enough to build up an appetite.

Heading back home, I heard driver after driver celebrating the new season by sharing their musical taste. Always rap or classic rock. Why do I never pass by a BMW dawdling at a red light, the melismatic witchery of Celine Dion wafting past open windows?

## WEDNESDAY

What do I want out of life? To be a little less arbitrary. I would like also to see stars actually glitter in the sky. I suspect that's something writers made up.

The sky can be minute after minute of delirious fun. I caused the moon to expand just before sitting down to begin this entry, out and out, until it covered a third of the sky. I stared and stared, but nothing else changed and I became bored.

In yesterday's entry I mentioned a co-worker. Her name is Libby—except not really—and most of the time she doesn't speak unless required. Meaning pleasantries and customer spiel. I find her passivity grating, but I'm a nice guy, so when I decided to grab lunch at Chipotle next door I asked my fellow sloggers if they wanted anything. Libby was in the back breaking down boxes when I approached her.

I asked and she wasted no time in replying. "No." Blunt, bland. Voice as pale as her face, as flat as her chest.

"I'm paying." Sugar, meet pot.

"No." A hint of a head shake.

My rumbling stomach, my plummeting blood sugar—all to blame. I had to say something, and as long as I kept it short and refrained from shouting, what harm would there be? I walked a few steps towards her and stopped. She placed the boxcutter on a nearby shelf and slowly turned to face me.

"You know you're allowed to say more than two words per sentence to non-customers," I spat out. "I know you probably feel self-conscious about your lisp, but we all have problems and we all do our best to deal with them. Obviously the people who hired you didn't think your voice was all that bad. So try a little more confidence. Maybe then you can make more sales and I won't be kicking your butt so badly in commissions."

I looked at her more intently than any man ever had, likely. Her eyes had widened and her cheeks had reddened, but not a peep in response.

"Right? Can you agree with that? Can you say it? Please. I'm asking you. Please. Pretty please. Say, 'I should speak up and increase my commissions.' If you say it, the chances of it actually coming to pass are increased."

I kept looking, seeking any indication that she was going to do anything other than breathe and blink. This look came over her…she was not intimidated, or amused, or confused or in any way overwhelmed by my outburst.

She straightened her posture. I noticed her shoulder blades jutting through her shirt fabric and wondered if she knew the ace she held in her hand.

"I won't say any of that," she announced, voice so loaded with menace that I briefly considered snatching the boxcutter from the shelf. "I'd much rather lock you in this room, then go up into the ceiling and carve a hole in one of those panels. Then I'd put my mouth over the hole and start speaking. More than I've ever said in here before, special words. Mississippi. Biscuits. Misfits, superstitious, fictitious, britches, shamanistic, sorceresses apprentice. On and on, till you drown."

I bought her a chicken and rice burrito. She seemed to appreciate that.

## THURSDAY

Bleak, grey...to me. Everyone else got to enjoy 80 degree weather.

Twice a month, give or take, I visit my parents. They only live an hour's drive away, and they've always been decent to me, so why not. Today of all days was their 27th anniversary, so right after work I hopped on the highway.

They live in a nice condo overseen by people who actually care about things like ground maintenance. It's a safe area, a bit quiet, and while it would send me to schizophrenia if I had to maintain a life there for more than a few months, the place is absolutely perfect for them.

Mother let me in and kissed me on both cheeks before even saying hello. She's that way, always. I took in the smell of a chicken and rice casserole—one of her go-to dishes.

"Mother," I said, half-aghast. "You mean to tell me Dad's making you cook on your anniversary?"

"Oh honey, he's always busy. He's locked himself in the office as usual." She threw up a hand to swat at the silliness.

I've yet to come out to my parents as a gay man, but I had no qualms telling my mother about my "peculiarities in perception." I didn't blurt it out—I waited until the third time it happened, when the bell rang at the conclusion of fourth-grade English class, a sound that watered the seeds implanted in every students soil. I watched as my classmates one by one grew at least a foot taller. I was the last student through the doors of the school, gaping at how Jessica Grandy's hair trailed behind her like a bridal gown.

I meant what I told you—I am not seeking treatment because society has convinced me that what I'm experiencing is wrong or whatever. I find it more invigorating than anything. While I've been fortunate to have not suffered any great detriment (or caused any to another person) because of this condition, I know very well that I'm due. So if I can somehow get to the bottom of this whole thing—I mean, it *has* to be a mental thing, I know for a fact there's no other option. If you think I'm lying, or exaggerating, fine. The select few I've told feel that way.

Except my mother. Though, I'm pretty sure she doesn't *really* believe my claims of spontaneous blobistic visions and discolored skin. Wonderful woman, however, she will never admit to herself any doubt in anything her only surviving child says or does.

My dad still doesn't know; I made mom promise never to tell him before I did—if I did—because I didn't want him to think any less of me. He and I have always had a decent, you-are-there-I-am-here-here-we-are father/son relationship. Acknowledgment equals respect to him. So I made sure to knock on his office door and announce my presence.

I spent some time watching the darling little woman responsible for my arrival as she darted around the kitchen space. "Need a hand?" I asked, hoping she wouldn't stop to see the smirk on my face.

"I have it all under control, sweetie. Why don't you sit down, you must be tired after being on your feet all day at work."

Not really, but I strolled over to the couch anyway. I'll never be a fan of their place—the ceilings are too tall for them. For anyone who isn't a pro basketball player, really. Or a stilts-fetishist.

It's also too bright. Not just the walls and the decor, but the lighting, how they aren't both blind.... I sat, hands in lap, and thought of the house I grew up in. It seemed so large, yet so comforting at the same time. We had the nicest yard on the block, thanks to mom, and she was so cool with letting us visit friends to play. She trusted us, and that's huge when you're a kid.

Lost in memories, I saw an amber swirl begin to form, a foot or so in front of my face. A few seconds later, I began to feel the swirl as well. A solid circle pressing between my shoulder blades, insistent and confident. A wordless lullaby.

Me on the couch, mom in the kitchen, dad in the office, all felt right. Almost.

I opened my eyes when I heard a door open. The swirl vanished. My father stood at the end of the hallway, eyes drooping and shoulders hunched. All that man does is read other people's words and speak other people's words.

"Twenty-seven years ago today," he muttered, scratching his nose, oblivious to my presence mere feet in front of him. Poor guy (ha). He's fond of making of what I have always assumed are jokes about balls attached to chains and whips in the hands of apron-clad shrews. He's either a master of the deadpan or one day he's going to beat his wife dead with a pan. I figure if that hasn't happened by anniversary 30, she's safe.

He took his standard chair and grunted in my direction. He hadn't shed work, sleeves rolled up and grey dress pants swishing.

"Dinner smells great!"

"What's that, sweetie?"

"I said dinner smells great!"

Three beams of light suddenly appeared across his forehead, end to end, almost like the lines on the road. Dad is a good man, just not a terribly interesting one. I gave up expecting much from him years ago, and we're both better off for it. When I graduated high school he asked what I wanted to do with my life. I thought for a few seconds, then explained my dream to become either a professional parachutist or a semi-professional parachute maker. "I really see parachutes in my future," I stressed.

My father believes I'm a lunatic. I'll present a decent counter-argument whenever I come across me.

He didn't speak much over dinner; if it weren't for the toast I initiated at the start, there would have been no mention at all of the anniversary. Mom did most of the talking, and even more of the listening. As is her way.

She saw me out, full of awe over my neat appearance. She's proud of her cultivated, *au courant* son. I'm proud of her, too. She's one of the *very few* people I've met that, when they say something, I don't wonder—what did they mean by *that*? She's as plain as the morning cup of coffee she'd surely die without.

Speaking of coffee...you wanted me to

talk about my dreams. Problem—my dreams are rare and unspectacular. Bland landscapes and colorless, motionless bodies.

I don't pray before bed. Instead, I stare at the print hanging on my bedroom wall—the Eiffel Tower, illuminated and immaculate. I want so badly to see it with my own eyes. Hopefully, it won't change.

Okay, technically it's Friday as I write this, but I've woken up three times in an hour already and I don't care to make a new entry yet. The sheets are wet, as is the pillowcase. I think I've been dreaming, but I can't be sure. The Topamax may be connected, as it's only day 4.

After I finished writing, I decided to pop my pill and play some Tetris online. I still wasn't tired, so on went the TV. *Frasier* rerun. The bon mots flew, the dog did something (or didn't), and it was a pre-Niles and Daphne episode, so it was good.

(I just want to say—I'm not one of those soup bowls for brains who think putting a will-they-won't-they couple together spells instant death for a TV show. *The Office* did it well. But *Frasier* shat the bed. The writing is somewhat to blame, but David Hyde Pierce deserves the brown crown. There do exist gay actors who can pull off het attraction, and work up a decent amount of chemistry with their pretend paramour, but he is just not among their ranks.)

Kelsey Grammar singing was my cue to call it a night. I was in bed barely one minute before I felt...ants marching around my bloodstream. I sat up and tried to regain my grip. Before I could feel too grateful to no longer have that insanely weird sensation, it was replaced by another one. It was as if I'd been worked over by hired goons for "failure of prompt payment." My chest and abdomen ached, my legs and arms sagged from

invisible weights, and my left eye started twitching.

But then—oh, wow. I was staring straight ahead, reminding myself over and over that no matter what was going on at the moment, it was not going to send me out of my mind or into my grave. I always leave the bedroom door open and the bathroom light on at night; it's my way of having a night light without feeling like I'm still eight years old. I stared past my door, greedily absorbing the glow, when images began to fall.

Somehow, the Tetris game I'd played and the *Frasier* episode I'd watched in the hour before bed combined. I sat, dumbfounded, as game pieces (each about the size of my TV screen) appeared in the air, the blocks made of images from the episode. They began near the ceiling and vanished just before touching the floor. None of them turned in mid-air. I might *still* be running if *that* had occurred.

FRIDAY

Rained again, but the drops splashed red everywhere. The ground, the cars, the streets, twas truly glorious. Spotted Drew and a mystery man again at lunch time, hands clasped as they said their goodbyes. It didn't make me upset at all; I was actually happy. They didn't care about anyone seeing them, which says a lot in this area especially. Feeling feverish, I began looking around, specifically for some local trash that might try and make trouble. I don't know what I would have done had I actually spotted someone, but I didn't, so it's irrelevant anyway.

I thought about the blood squirting

from my own heart, just the vision, and felt wobbly. Perhaps I should be more grateful that I *don't* run this show.

Last day of the work week usually goes agonizingly slow, no matter how much foot traffic. The walkers outnumbered the talkers today, but I still made a few nice hauls. Poor Libby only struck fool's gold once, to a blonde woman in one of the tightest skirts I've ever seen. Throw in the fact a young child was hopping and bopping at her side, and I was more than fine with letting Libby have *that* one.

(I do, here and there, experience attraction to a woman. But I could never love one. I've yet to see a female who displays the colors of the more fascinating males.)

I have a bit of a bone to pick with you, sir. I've been sitting here checking out the side effects of Topamax, and imagine my amusement/bemusement upon seeing this: "weight loss, confused thinking, diarrhea, dry mouth, sensory distortion."

Are you playing a prank on me or do you just not pay attention? I'm half-joking here, as I don't actually expect this stuff to help, but I hope my next prescription isn't so ironic.

Voice in my head be damned, I even went online to read other people's experiences with Topamax and apparently the "confused thinking" is pretty common? "Dopamax" is a popular nickname? This is *acceptable*? Thus, my options: experience random illusions of mysterious origin, *or*, twitch and drool as I try to remember how to put on pants. What a racket you guys have going.

Of course, I found myself lost in the rabbit hole of side effects stories on the internet till dinner time. The woman in

Nebraska who had to be taken off Ambien after waking up in her backyard with three fingernails ripped off almost made me chew through my Ethernet cable!

## SATURDAY

These words are being written on a slab of raw meat! A cow must be attempting to communicate with me! How droll. If you've ever read the second Harry Potter book, you understand that by doing as you ask, I may very well be giving my soul over to a malevolent milk-giving force.

Every Saturday morning, I drive out to the park. My mission is simple (3-5 miles on foot) and it is almost always accomplished. I believe most people, if they take the time and effort to maintain a healthy diet, only require one day of rigorous exercise. Of course everyone's different…but honestly, this country does not need so many gyms. Think of the time and money people would save if they just understood their bodies better.

The air felt soupy. Yet, I felt no more or less tired at the end of walk than usual. It took me a little longer, through no fault of my own. A solid week of gorgeous temps means increased park presence, which means *stragglers*. People without real *purpose*, just there to enjoy the weather while moving around. You may as well stay home and mow the lawn! Some of us have purpose. Now move!

The attractiveness ratio between men and women in this town is all out of whack. Cute young guys abound—even if their attire makes it plain they don't quite see themselves that way—but the women. So many of them are made up and over. Perfumed with an emphasis on the *fume*.

Stretch marks and elbow moles implied.

A scruff in a "Hank Jr" rag-to-be smirked at me as we crossed paths. I briefly considered swinging back around and slapping his butt…maybe even cupping a cheek…Americans aggravate me so much. But where else can I even be right now? The future, though. I could live in a country with couth and class. I could live in a country that would force me to learn another language! I could learn to look inoffensive in a beret!

It's not unusual to bump into people I actually want to bump into, people I actually know. Usually I can get away with some eye contact and a head nod, a word or two depending on…a number of factors. But then there's times like today, when I meet an old friend.

"Hey! What's going on? Been awhile. How do I look? No, seriously, tell me how I look. Do I look weird?"

"I told you before, that's gone. It must have been a phase or something."

"Yeah, sure. Gone like it was never here, because it never was. You're a funny guy."

And I had to laugh, for at that moment my friend turned into a stick figure. Headband and all.

Nearing the south entrance of the park I geared up to jog the last fifty or so feet when a familiar voice put the kibosh on that plan.

"Hello, shoe boy."

I half-turned to the left and saw Drew, standing in the grass, grasping car keys and anticipating my reaction. Oh great! My heart and stomach switched places. How unlikely was *this*? He and I had never run into one another outside of the shopping plaza. Somehow, I resisted clawing at the air. I credit the cheerleading squad gathered in my chest.

"Hey, hi!" Ugh, I think I scared a small bird away with my pitch. "What's going on?"

"It's my nephew's sixth birthday. I'm helping out with the decorating." He pointed to a pavilion twenty feet or so from where we stood, near the lake. I saw a few women blowing up balloons and unrolling streamers.

"A nice sunny Saturday surrounded by kids," I said, in as neutral a tone as I could manage.

"Well, my sister owes me one for this. Just thinking about the possibilities will get me through the whole ordeal." He smiled, all thirty-two in attendance. I wanted to grab his words before they dissipated, fold them up and slip them into my pockets.

Did I detect a glimmer in those gorgeous hazel-green eyes? Or was that just a reflection? Briefly, I considered opening up.

"Hey Drew, I know this might sound a little weird, and I would *not* blame you if you refused to believe a single word I'm about to say, but this week at work all of the numbers on the register keypad disappeared while I was ringing up a fat lady's order. And what's weirder, I didn't even flinch because things like that have been happening for years!"

He'd be totally sympathetic and interested, right? Right? Since I couldn't guarantee his response, I bit my tongue.

Many motorcycles on the road today. All of them remind me of my brother. He owned two—one red, one blue, and he called them the closest to children he would ever have. He loathed cars and rarely drove the one our parents gave him upon graduation. He was a musclebound sweetheart beloved by most. Including me. When I was seven or eight, I wanted to pack a bindle and run up and away to the moon. I told him, figuring that he'd just laugh at me. Instead, he wished me luck and gave me a high-five.

The man on the moon was probably my first crush. Or Michael J. Fox.

Oreos and milk for dinner. Hardly healthy, but I haven't eaten all day. Hey, heavy *heavy* confession time, one week I ate naught but Burger King fries. To (mostly) quote a (mostly) man—"Bang on my chest if you think I'm perfect, Dorothy."

I lied earlier. At the beginning of the week. I don't own Hugo Boss shoes. They're just Clarks. Purchased at a discount, too. Very nice, but a discerning eye wouldn't be fooled. Probably you weren't. Being an accredited man of the mind and all.

One more day. Hopefully I have not doomed the world by opening the door for Lord Moosalot.

## SUNDAY

Everywhere are gems, encased in steel, buried underneath dirt and clay and weeds. With time and ingenuity, it's possible to find more than just a few of them. Fanfare upon discovery! But! Is all the effort worth it? And no, that is *not* a rhetorical question; only a lazy-brained individual would interpret it as such.

Visited a relatively recent downtown addition known as True Blue for a sublime breakfast: brie with strawberries! *Bon appetit*! Good crowd, but I still fear the place won't last. I lack faith in the populace.

The ground *felt* strange. New one. I suspected that if I knelt down and pressed on the sidewalk, it would have broken underneath my fingertips like styrofoam. Am I going from visual to tactile abnormalities? I jogged the rest of the way home, a block and

a half, with hardly any company, save for an affectionate young couple waiting for a light to change.

I'd like to fall in love. I might even like the way it feels. Not until I'm past thirty years old though. Romantic love is infamous for making smart people behave stupidly, so I figure with the proper training, I can guard against the standard pitfalls and snares.

Based on observation and hearsay, here's what I know so far.

Ask a person out (or get asked out). The first date doesn't go well, that's that. If it does, though, a second date shall follow. On and on, until passion has its ways. Unless you've lucked into some of that silly fluffy stuff (soulmates and such, yuck), the connection is as doomed as a child in Willy Wonka's factory. After the termination of the relationship, at least one of the parties involved copes by insisting that what they felt was not *truly* romantic love. They endure self-reflection. They adjust accordingly, becoming more discerning, their assessments harsher. They close up a chamber of their heart just to survive.

(By the by, I was indeed taking a jab at you earlier. You indulge in rhetorical questions too frequently for me to take you as seriously as the letters appearing after your name insist I should. What's college, after all. I dropped out after two years. My academic performance was fine, I got on well with my peers, but wouldn't you know—the environment just wasn't stimulating enough. The last two months I was having illusions at a rate of three a day.)

So there it is, a full week. Very curious what we can make of this. Maybe time to pack another bindle? The man on the moon has aged very well.

# HOLDING SAMPSON

## TOM WELLER

Sampson was an accident, a product of a fused blossom, probably, and storm water reaching more roots than leaves, of unusually hot, sunny days and unseasonably crisp nights. Nature, not science, not any human hands, birthed Sampson. Claire called it a miracle. Claire might have been right.

Among the six scraggly plants we had growing in our single bed along the garage, Sampson stood out like a diamond in a coal bin even early on. While the other tomatoes looked like green acorns emerging from the vines, Sampson already looked like a green fist, the punch of a monster. "Well, look at that," Claire said nodding toward green Sampson as we worked side-by-side weeding our small patch.

"Ain't that somthin'," I said, and reached toward green Sampson just as Claire reached for green Sampson, our hands moving parallel to each other, as if we were each a funhouse mirror for the other, as if the same need had been born in each of us in the exact same second.

It felt good, moving together, just Claire and me. That's how it had always been, just Claire and me. No kids. Not for lack of trying. Not for lack of heartbreak. But Claire and I didn't move together as much as we used to. Maybe that's just what fifty-odd years of marriage do to people. All the little slights and hurt feelings, the I-forgots and the never-noticings, the noticing-but-not-saying-thank-yous, maybe those all accumulate over the years and gum up the works like tar in a transmission. Maybe that buildup bogs down the whirring gears of love.

As days lengthened then receded tomatoes grew. From green to pink to red they went, fat with sunshine and rain, swelling up faster than a black eye, their flesh like a good handshake, warm and firm. And still Sampson put the other tomatoes to shame. One day he was three times their size, the next day five, the next maybe eight, maybe ten. We worried he'd be too much for the vine, so Claire built a hammock out of old pantyhose and cut-and-twisted wire hangers, something to take the weight off the vine, something to keep Sampson out of the dirt.

"How big do you think he'll get," Claire asked me as June faded into July.

"As big as he wants, looks like."

The others were easy. He's a pretty red. Pick 'im. That one too, red as a cardinal. Pick 'im , and that one, and that one. We'd stretch the bottom of our t-shirts into makeshift baskets and fill them with tomatoes for dinner. Extras we'd take to the neighbors, leave them on porch railings, in mailboxes, anonymous kindness. But when do you pick a giant tomato? How do you know when it's become as big as it wants to be? Claire and I wore this conundrum like wet sweaters, questions heavy and irritating and impossible to ignore. Evenings, I'd crouch on my hands and knees in the dirt, one ear pressed to Sampson while Claire stood over me, her face pinched in thought. I'd flick my index finger against Sampson two times, three, four, five. He'd make a sound like a tennis ball meeting concrete.

"What do you think?" Claire would say.

"I don't know."

"Maybe one more day?"

"Yeah. One more day." Claire would offer me a hand up. I'd refuse her help. Man pride. My bones would groan as I stood. And the next evening my knees would be back in the damp soil of our small garden plot, and in the cool of Claire's shadow I'd flick Sampson, bigger and redder than he had been the night before.

The dream was just a voice blooming in my head at 3:00 a.m., a rumbling in the night-black atmosphere still thick with summer humidity. The voice sounded like Charlton Heston, but it wasn't Charlton Heston. I recognized the voice from its first note the way some people recognize bird songs.

The voice said, "I'm as big as I want to be."

The voice said, "Now."

Claire was already in the garden when I arrived. She stood next to Sampson. The soft soil of the garden bed filled the gaps between her bare toes. "You heard it too," she said. Claire did the honors. No ceremony, just a quick tug. Just like that it was done. And just like that it had begun.

We walked back to the house side by side, Sampson riding in the basket of Claire's raised nightgown, our bare feet padding like cats' paws across the backyard grass.

The newspaperman seemed to be part cricket. His black hair was slicked back with pomade. He had beady, dark eyes. He hopped around the kitchen, chirping about finding the best light, chirping questions: "What variety? Grown from seed? How long? Any more?" The camera hanging from his neck swung along with his movements.

The morning after we picked Sampson we weighed him. While Claire brewed coffee and scrambled eggs in the kitchen, I rummaged around in the garage until I unearthed the old grocery scale Claire and I had bought at a flea market many years ago for reasons neither one of us could recall. Sampson looked regal sitting in the chrome basket of the scale, like an emperor in a gleaming chariot. Ten pounds, eight ounces.

This was big, call-the-newspaper big.

The newspaperman scooped Sampson up from the table and put him on the counter then picked him back up again. He hopped in a tight little circle. "Fertilizer? Secrets?" He picked Sampson up. He put Sampson down. He waved his hands at me like a man trying to pluck dandelion fluff from the air. "Would you mind getting up? Stand behind the tomato. Thanks. There you go. Great. Oh. You too, Claire. It's Claire, right? Yep. That's it. Great. The loving couple behind the amazing tomato. That's the story. Just great. Perfect. Maybe not. Try picking the tomato up." I scooped Sampson up in both hands, presenting him to the camera like a priest making an offering. I felt his weight in my forearms, in my wrists. "That's better. Maybe. Claire? Claire, right? Get in there too, Claire."

Claire squeezed in closer. Her left shoulder leaned into my right shoulder, the way it used to when we walked through winter winds, Claire searching for warmth, me hoping my heat was enough. I felt her hand skittering under mine, looking for a hold on Sampson. I let my right hand fall away. Claire's hand moved in to take its place. My load lightened. I felt Sampson's warmth against my palm. I felt Claire's breath against my neck. Claire shifted her hand. Our fingers touched. I felt movement in my palm. At first I thought it was my pulse, my heartbeat. Then I realized it was coming from Sampson. Ba-dum, Ba-dum, Ba-dam. I felt it in my palm, steady and regular as a marching cadence. Ba-dum. Ba-dum. It matched my heartbeat. I felt Claire breathing next to me. In and out, in and out, the tickle of air against my neck, a feeling

like electricity, electricity sparking in perfect time with my heartbeat, in perfect time with Sampson. "Do you feel it?" Claire whispered.

I mouthed *I do.*

"That's it. Perfect. Now smile. Perfect. Don't move."

We stood still, but even bathed in the white light of the camera's flash we never stopped moving. Breath and pulse and heartbeats, moving, me and Claire and Sampson, all moving together.

It's hard to say exactly how it started. Maybe it started right after the newspaperman left and I pulled Claire to me, my right hand resting on the small of Claire's back, Claire's fingertips skipping along my left forearm, tongues of fire blooming in our eyes. Or maybe it started earlier. Maybe it started with the flash of the newspaperman's camera or with the tug that freed Sampson from the vine, or maybe it started with the planting of a seed, an act of hope and faith. Or maybe it started many, many years ago with the first joke Claire ever told me, the first time we laughed together.

I can say how it ended: Claire and I sweaty and naked on the kitchen floor, our limbs jumbled together like a game of pick-up-sticks, my arms and legs, hollow, numb, electricity crackling in my chest.

As soon as the newspaperman left, Claire and I made love on the kitchen floor. Mouth on mouth, tongue on tongue, the sharing of breath, we took our time. When we finished, I stayed on the kitchen floor, tangled with Claire, and watched the slow rising and falling of her chest as she drifted off to sleep.

*Amazing* read the caption below our picture in the paper the next day. It's a good picture, black and white. Claire wears her white hair like a crown of clouds. My eyes sparkle, black as shale. Sampson, a slick grey, steadfast and pretty as polished steel, claims the foreground. It's an amazing picture.

*Amazing* said the neighbors who came to the house asking to see Sampson. Some would ask the same questions the newspaperman had: Variety? Fertilizer? Secrets? Some would just talk weather and sports. They all told as stories about their tomatoes, how they had once, not too far back, grown one almost as big as Sampson, maybe bigger, how they and their tomato probably should have been in the newspaper, too. They all said Sampson was amazing. And every night, when the people had all gone home, Claire and I made love on the kitchen floor. And every night before we fell asleep on that floor, curled together like a couple of pups, we'd look at each other and say together "Amazing," a word shared, a prayer of thanks.

The kitchen remained crowded even after the neighbors stopped coming by. Sampson took up some space, and me and Claire, of course, and stray dirty dishes lingering in the sink. Memories of having spent the last four nights making love to Claire in the kitchen filled every other square inch. Naked bodies dappled in moonlight and shadow. Sampson vibrating on the table. Claire's heart beating against my chest. Claire's touch clung to me like pine tar; I could not wash it from my skin. The memories swirled around me, everywhere, a flock of ghosts whispering lyrics to old love songs.

"Do you see it?" Claire said when she brought me my coffee. I sat in my chair at the kitchen table. Sampson, perched on a silver tray, sat in the center of the table, as dignified as a Thanksgiving turkey.

I stared at Sampson. "He's different," I said. Claire sat down across from me, and we both stared at Sampson, a couple of gypsies exploring a crystal ball.

"Different. But how?" Claire leaned in toward Sampson.

I reached out and touched Sampson. His flesh gave where it did not give before, a feeling like touching a package of raw meat. I waited for it, waited. The ghosts swirling around me stilled, shushed each other quiet. Finally it came, fainter, maybe slower than before, but it was still there, vibrations in my fingertips. "He's dying," I said.

"I guess we always knew this would come."

We both knew what we would do next. We both knew we didn't have a choice.

It was about Sampson. It was about letting Sampson be Sampson. It was about respect. It was about thanks.

We started by moving Sampson and his silver platter to the kitchen counter, higher ground, closer to God. Claire and I took up positions behind the counter. Shoulder to shoulder, we looked down upon Sampson's failing red flesh. Claire took my right hand in her left. Electricity. I turned to look at Claire. Claire turned to look at me. She nodded. The ghosts of our love making quieted, swallowed their lyrics about red roses and true hearts and blue dreams of yesterday, swallowed all their I-can't-stops and their I do-do-dos. I lowered my head, retreated to the silence of my skull, waited for the right words to come to me.

I raised my eyes toward Sampson. I felt his vibration, his hum, weaker still, felt it moving down the counter, through the floorboards, and nesting in the bottom of my feet. I spoke: "Amazing." Claire's hand tightened around mine.

I tipped my head back, looked at the ceiling. "Amazing." Louder this time, more bass. The dishes in the sink rattled.

I squeezed Claire's hand and raised my arm, raised both of our arms. I looked to Claire. She looked to me. "Amazing," I said. The ghosts of our lovemaking ceased their swirling, drifted into tight rows behind Claire and I. Claire mouthed a word to me. I think she mouthed *more*. Sampson deserved more. We all deserved more.

"Amazing grace," I said, "How sweet the sound."

Claire joined in with me, her voice like caramel, rich and smooth. "That saved a wretch like me," we said together. We kept our joined hands in the air. We swayed side-to-side, slow, easy.

"I once was lost, but now I'm found." The ghosts of our lovemaking joined in, a chorus of whispers floating under our voices, "was blind but now I see." That was as much as I knew, so I took a deep breath and circled back to the start.

"Amazing." I punched the word, let it out like a command, and everybody stayed right with me. Me, Claire, the ghosts, note for note, breath for breath, together, "grace how sweet the sound that saved a wretch like me." We went through the whole thing three times. And then we stopped.

With my free hand I pulled a knife from the dish drainer. I grabbed the good knife, the one Claire was sensitive about me using, the one that sliced bread so thin you could read your newspaper through it. I passed the knife to my right hand. Together, Claire and I took up the knife and raised it above our head. A burst of sunlight reflected off the blade, twinkled above Sampson like his very own star. The ghost chorus whispered again behind us: "Amazing grace, how sweet the sound…." The vibrations in the soles of my feet stilled.

A nod to Claire was all it took. The cut was guillotine quick, clean as surgery. A disk of Sampson's flesh, slick with seeds and juice, lay on the tray. The ghosts whispered on: "I once was lost, but now I'm found…." Together Claire and I cut the slice of Sampson in half. Together we lay the good knife on the tray next to Sampson. Separately we each picked up half of the slice. Together we entwined our arms. Together each fed the other. Tomato seeds, slick as mercury, dribbled down our chins.

Claire and I spent the rest of the morning eating Sampson. Most of the ghosts of our lovemaking retreated. They moved into the cabinets we seldom opened; they moved under the refrigerator. One disappeared down the sink drain. Many of them receded right into the walls, ghosts joining plaster and lathe. But a few of the ghosts joined us at the kitchen table, kept us company while we finished Sampson. They whispered while we ate.

They whispered the first joke Claire had ever told me, many, many years ago: "Why didn't the skeleton go to the dance? Because he didn't have any body to dance with."

They whispered a joke I would tell Claire months in the future in a dimly lit hospital room: "How does the ocean say goodbye? It doesn't. It just waves." The last joke I would ever tell Claire.

But mostly, they whispered "Amazing." Claire and I filled our mouths with the goodness of tomato, flesh and seeds and juice, and listened to those few ghosts whispering "Amazing" over and over and over again.

# THROAT FULL OF PIGEON

## CHRIS KURIATA

*That's him*, Bianca thought, watching the old man from over top of her menu.

She ignored her husband and son as they consulted price and health requirements to determine who was allowed to order what.

A fresh pint slid across the restaurant's elegant, oak bar into the old man's hands. From Bianca's table on the other side of the dining room, she could see his Adam's apple rapidly bob up and down like a cocooned insect struggling to emerge.

*Jesus Christ, that's absolutely him.*

Thirty-seven years had passed since grade four, since Bianca last saw Pige. She remembered him being old even then, over seventy. The teachers would invite him to class, where he'd park his long janitorial broom against the chalkboard and tell the children about events he'd witnessed firsthand, like The Great Depression, or World War I (which Pige still referred to as "The Great War").

Genetics, Bianca told herself, explained how Pige could be over a hundred years old and still sucking down pints at the Mansion House on Wednesday evening. Genetics were why one person got lung cancer in their thirties (her mother) and another chain-smoked across an entire century (you-know-who).

Although Bianca thought about Pige often over the years, she always assumed him long dead, jumbled bones in a rotted suit. She never considered what she might do if they ever ran into one another, never thought she'd be given the opportunity.

*This is once in a lifetime.* Bianca lowered her menu. *Don't squander it.*

Lawrence wanted the prime rib, knowing full well the cut of meat would pale in comparison to the one they enjoyed in Banff Springs on their honeymoon. He ordered this steak specifically to compare it to that perfect meal, never tiring of recalling that magical evening when their love was young. Their son Oscar—after much hemming and hawing—chose the popcorn shrimp and was delighted by his platter of fried breading. Bianca professed to be "not hungry," ordering the house soup and salad. Without taking a single bite, she excused herself from the table and followed the man she'd been watching right into the bathroom.

Pige played a one-man band at the urinal. He moaned, cracked his knees, and farted before the first splash of urine hit the enamel.

Bianca saddled up beside him, casually hiking the hem of her dress as though positioning herself at the urinal was the most natural thing in the world. She didn't actually have to piss, which was a good thing since she didn't know how to pinch her anatomy to focus her stream. She still carried the memory of that high school bush fire when her friends dropped their jeans and expertly tinkled their Labatt Blue piss onto the fire to the simultaneous disgust and delight of the boys, who cheered as the red wood crackled and steamed. When Bianca's turn came, she bowed her legs to direct her crotch at the fire but her stream was weak and the urine flowed backwards, running up the crack of her ass where it sputtered out between her cheeks, soaking the jeans pooled around her ankles. She sat in her damp all night, certain she smelled and that everyone was disgusted with her. She never attempted freestanding urination again.

At the urinal beside Pige, she ghost pissed, wanting him to make first contact. Let's see if he recognized her.

In her peripheral vision, she watched Pige shake his withered cock and spit a long rope of tobacco colored hork into the basin. She could smell the cigarette tar stuck to his teeth.

"S'cuse me," he said, bumping his shoulder into hers. Bianca realized she failed to follow proper men's room etiquette. Two men at the urinal were supposed to leave a space between one another. Men wanted the comfort of distance to reassure them some weirdo wasn't going to sneak a peek at their wiener.

At the sink, Pige twisted the faucets but kept his hands out of the water. He only made a show of washing for her benefit. Otherwise, he would have barreled out the door back to his stool and handed the bartender money for his next drink with piss splattered hands.

Bianca flushed her unused urinal and hurried to join Pige at the sinks before he wandered away. She tried to think of a way to break the ice, drop a hint to their former acquaintance.

He denied her eye contact. Ignoring the prominent NO SMOKING stickers plastered between the mirrors, Pige stuck a half-smoked butt into his mouth and inhaled deeply. The tiny embers lying dormant in the black stump sprung to life, turning the tip bright red and feeding thick smoke to pour out of his nostrils—twin plumes like from a dragon's snout.

"I kept the truck engine running," Pige said, still not making eye contact, not even in the mirror. "I knew you were comin' so I kept her warm for you. Shall we go?"

Bianca took a moment to think of Lawrence and Oscar. She had the family credit card in her purse. If she abandoned her boys to climb into Pige's truck would they have enough money to pay for Lawrence's prime rib and Oscar's popcorn shrimp? With drinks, they were probably looking at a fifty-seven dollar tab. As far as she was concerned, if Lawrence didn't have fifty-seven dollars tucked into the reserve of his wallet he deserved to wash dishes to pay off his bill. She hooked her arm into Pige's.

"Let's go."

The headlights on Pige's pickup were dark. The engine was stone cold, having cooled down for hours while Pige sat at the bar. He lied to her about keeping the engine running. He had no idea she was coming. Bianca felt crushed.

*What the fuck, too late to turn back now.*

Pige drove fast out of the parking lot. The steering wheel handled slippery and the back of his pickup fishtailed. The inside of the truck smelled sour, like neglected laundry. Bianca wondered if Pige was living in his truck, and began wiping dust from the dashboard, tidying up for him.

She recognized the streets they rumbled down, even though all the business had changed. At the intersection, Bianca remembered there used to be a crossing guard, Miss Milne, whose sister-in-law Mrs. Milne taught grade one. Even as a nine year old, Bianca wondered if the crossing guard resented her sister-in-law, considering her a bigger success inside the school building while she stood in the rain waving a red cardboard octagon at cars to let children pass.

Pige rocketed through the traffic lights. Bianca squirmed to see him drive so recklessly. Despite his cool demeanor, he was anxious to get her back to their old spot. She turned her head so he wouldn't see her smile.

The school was long gone. Built in 1958, the entire brick structure had been torn down for the valuable land located in the centre of the city. An entire sub-division

of little houses—all touching like buns baked close together in a pan—covered the field where Bianca once learned arithmetic and the sanitized history of early fur traders, while Pige roamed the halls replacing burned out lights and sweeping the floor.

The missing school left a hole in Bianca's heart. She reached for Pige's hand, but he jerked away, a man on the move, no time for sentimentality.

Squatting on his knees, Pige groped through the bushes and azaleas of the community garden until he found the bottle of whiskey he kept stashed there. He gave himself an eye-opener, then pressed the glass bottle to Bianca's lips. The alcohol burned going down her throat, and was pulpy like freshly-squeezed orange juice, full of bits of backwashed food. There was even a tooth sucked out of Pige's rotten gums rattling at the bottom of the bottle.

After he stuffed his bottle back into the garden, he grabbed Bianca's wrist and tugged her along like Peter Pan guiding Wendy out the window into the London night. Bianca knew so long as she held on, he would fly her to the land she had long been dreaming of. She dug her nails into Pige's wrist, committing herself to not letting go.

They came to a dim house in the middle of the street. Pige barely kicked the front door before the hinges swung wide open, eager to welcome him inside. The door jamb looked gnawed, the result of multiple locks having been kicked open. As Bianca brushed past the splintered wood she counted the locks and chains—six of them. At one time, someone tried securing this door, but Pige kicked it open so many times they gave up. A beaded curtain would do a better job keeping uninvited visitors out.

Fried onions hung in the air. The

lingering smell assaulted Bianca's nostrils. The onions were partially burned, left in the frying pan too long. Likely, the occupant of the house got confused and forgot about them simmering on the stove. Bianca shook her head. One day, this inattentive cooking would burn the house down. This fact relieved any guilt she felt about trespassing. She didn't bother wiping her feet on the mat.

An elderly woman draped in a crusted bathrobe sat in the living room watching TV, the volume cranked so loud the mesh over the ten cent speakers vibrated like the set was stuffed full of crickets. Her feet were propped up, and yellow toenails burst through the end of her nylons. Bianca spotted an out of season artificial Christmas tree beside the Chesterfield. Two dusty gifts waited beneath the painted leaves. The old woman must have placed them there for grandchildren, maybe as far back as three Christmases ago.

The old woman knew the drill. As soon as Pige snapped the TV off, she shuffled away to bed, obedient as an old dog. She cast her eyes over Bianca as she shambled past. Bianca jutted out her chin and held the old woman's gaze. The creaky bitch was trying to make her feel small, not worthy of Pige's company.

*She's jealous.*

With the living room empty, Bianca followed Pige into the closet tucked between the living room and the kitchen. She relaxed once the door closed behind them. This space felt comfortable. Familiar. Pige didn't need to tell her, she already knew the closet occupied the exact same space the janitor closet had when the old school still existed. How perfect the house designers decided to put a closet on this exact same location. It was almost as though the entire subdivision had been built around this space with Pige in mind.

"It smells just the same." Bianca wasn't trying to flatter Pige. The old woman's closet smelled like dirty water from a mop bucket mixed with the lemon-scented saw dust Pige used to sprinkle over the children's throw up. Bianca felt vibrations humming in the floor. This space retained its special quality, whether enclosed in a school or an old lady's house. Here was Pige's temple, and Bianca was thankful to be in his presence once again. She got into position on her knees and said *ah*.

The tips of Pige's fingers were just how Bianca remembered them—all rough and fuzzy like Velcro. They danced across her tongue, and depending where he touched, the sensation became different.

On the tip of her tongue, his fingers tickled. Bianca giggled, and tilted her head back, encouraging him to push deeper into her mouth.

On the middle of her tongue, his fingers burned. Fumes filled her sinuses, clearing her breathing as effectively as a tablespoon of fresh horseradish. Her eyes watered, but Bianca knew to wait out this momentary discomfort. The burning would evaporate, and the new sensation would be so soothing.

"Take a good breath," Pige said before pushing his fingers to the very back of her tongue, where the red bumpy skin sloped into her throat. He moved his hand like an expert, able to press on this sensitive spot without making Bianca retch. Long ago, his fingers and her gag reflex reached a friendly agreement, and he leaned forward, shoving his arm deeper into her mouth.

Buried in her throat, Pige's fingers

tasted sweeter than the most syrupy baklava. Bianca closed her eyes, savouring each new sensation as he strummed her from deep inside. Thirty-seven miserable years had passed since she last enjoyed his touch. The absence added up to a wasted lifetime.

Her mind flittered back to watching nature videos in bed with Oscar before tucking him in. They saw deer spraying themselves with urine to be more attractive to mates, and Oscar roared with laughter, astonished to see true nature wasn't like Disney cartoons, but full of cruelty, and killing, and fucking. Next, they watched a snake unhinge his jaws to swallow a sweet rabbit whole.

"Is the rabbit alive the whole time it's being eaten?" Oscar asked, sounding concerned.

Bianca pulled the heavy sheets from his chin so he wouldn't sweat in the night. "I think the rabbit knows it's caught, so he closes his eyes and goes to sleep, that way he can pass away relaxed and at peace instead of thrashing around and suffering."

Back in Pige's temple, Bianca wondered if she could learn to stretch her mouth like a snake. Without her pesky jaw, Pige could reach deeper into her throat where the buds would be even sweeter.

She was about to ask Pige if the old woman had a hammer close by, when he withdrew his arm from her mouth and wiped his fingers on his overalls.

"What are you doing?"

His truck keys jingled. Time to get back in his pickup and look for the next spot of action. He didn't even offer her a ride back to the restaurant.

This wasn't right. Bianca waited too long for the sweet touch of Pige at the back of her throat to let him disappear so

abruptly. She never told anyone about their relationship, fearing they'd call her stupid for desiring the touch of a creepy old man. They didn't know what it was like to miss such a vital part of her childhood. Maybe if other men had touched her as majestically as Pige she could have forgotten him, but no man in her life, not even Lawrence attempted to be so intimate. Pige was clearly the wrong man, maybe he was even a bad man, but no one gave her such sweetness. How dare anyone make her feel ashamed for her desire?

"You can't go."

Pige's knees cracked loud as dropped eggs. Standing up, he bumped his head into the sloped ceiling, putting a dent in the plaster and creating a short rain of chalky dust. He seemed to have grown too big for the closet, and his elbows beat against the walls as claustrophobia took hold.

"S'cuse me," Pige said. "I left the engine running. I need to get there before the gas tank runs out."

He moved forward, expecting Bianca to step aside, but she pinned her arm across the door and repeated, as a command this time, "You can't go."

Lawrence and Oscar would wait for her with open arms no matter how long she stayed away. Pige's attention was more mercurial. If she let him drip through her fingers, there was no telling the next time she would see him again. When she was fifty? Sixty? When she was dead?

Like most people, Bianca knew better how to give advice than to follow it. When young girls at the office confessed their emotional dilemmas, Bianca advised them, "You see something you want, you grab hold and sink your teeth into it." She granted permission. In the cramped closet with Pige, she realized she spent all those years giving that advice not for the girls, but for her own benefit, in preparation for this moment.

She lunged at his arm, twisting his hand, feeling the tendons snap and his wrist crumble, before driving his fingers right down her throat. Truck keys smashed against her mouth, breaking a few chips off her front teeth, but her tongue swiftly pushed the keys into her cheek, catching them before they tumbled down her throat and choked her.

Pige tried pulling back, but her mouth was like quicksand. The harder he struggled, the more secure Bianca took hold. Her broken teeth found his knuckles easily, wedging between the joints, popping the bones apart. Separating the skin took more effort, but once Bianca tore through the elasticity Pige's fingers bounced past her tonsils and deep into her throat.

She didn't make an emotional goodbye. Abandoning Pige as his ancient body went into shock, she closed the closet door behind her. Let him sleep it off, out of sight of the old woman.

Outside, Bianca fished the truck keys from her cheek and tossed them into the garden beside the whiskey bottle, where Pige stood a good chance of finding them again. She wouldn't steal his filthy truck. That thing was a death trap. She doubted she could drive it five blocks without spinning off into a crash.

Instead, she gave hitchhiking a try. Why not? She had all her fingers, and since she didn't bite her nails, her thumb ended in a beautifully curved red nail, as smooth as a beetle's back. Someone would surely stop to pick up the owner of such a mesmerizing thumb.

As she walked down the vacant road, badly needing to use the washroom, Bianca flexed her throat muscles to hold Pige's

fingers pressed against her sweet spot. It took great concentration to balance his fingers there, a combination of physical and mental stamina. Spit built up, threatening to cut off her air, so Bianca leaned forward and drooled a red trail along the asphalt.

Bianca knew sooner or later, she would have to swallow and doing so would remove Pige's fingers from her throat forever. *How long can I remain mute?* Not everyone needed to talk. They learned sign language, or typed shit on their phone. As she bent over to drain more spit from her throat, she decided she could keep from swallowing for a long time. After all, so long as Lawrence and Oscar knew she loved them, what could she possibly have to say that was so goddam important?

# VERGING ON BLUE

## Michelle Willms

Rule One: Everyone is a sucker, and every moment, an opportunity.

It's what my father used to say. He attended Yale, and in his first year studying law, he felt the coveted shoulder-tap from the blue-blooded Skull and Bones Secret Society boys. I'm not supposed to know that and neither are you, so forget I said anything. Actually, remember it if you want to. I only know about the elitist group because at one of my parents' dinner parties, I overheard Dad telling a fellow Skull-Boner about his initiation, which involved getting shat on by all the other members. Metaphorically speaking, nothing's changed. And if Dad's stupid enough to blab about Skull and Bones in front of his ten-year-old kid while snorting lines, too whited-out to notice his own boy in the room, then what do I care who knows? Edward Hall. Skull and Bones. Spread the word.

Rule Two: Pay attention to detail.

Back then, life was silver spoons full of fish eggs, champagne flutes full of social lubricant, and D-cups full of Mom's new boobs—a gift to Dad on his fifty-second birthday. *Honk. Honk.* Why not his fiftieth birthday, Mom? And why don't people stick with significant milestones anymore? I asked Mom that, too. She smiled because she knew I was mocking her and her stupid plastic jugs.

I love my mom. The woman was a beautiful closet-drinker who was never sure of herself. Smart woman if you really got to know her. But tolerated a lot from Dad. Affairs. Turn a blind eye. That kind of stuff. I don't judge her. I can't anymore. She's dead.

I'm sure if she were still alive, she'd wear a big ol' scarf and hat during wintertime in New York, she'd take up our offer to stay in our guest room forever, and she'd have her boob reduction so she could live back in the A-day. Back in the A-day, she didn't have shoulder and neck issues. Back in the A-day, she didn't feel quite so rejected when Dad didn't come home at night. And for the record, I only know her former bra size because stupid rich women always pry (even when kids are within earshot), asking what size a woman used to be.

Mom died in her sleep seven years ago—blood clot in her brain. The ol' man's still kicking around. He's eating up his big pension and juicing the stock market. I invited him to enjoy the smells of cinnamon and pine with my wife and me during Christmas last year, but he said he didn't have time.

No time. Right. Have a good life buddy—that's what I say. I hope the poor hooker he picks up on Christmas Eve sets the hotel alarm clock for 3 AM, then duct tapes it to his head after he passes out. I promise you, I'm not crying on the inside. The only thing he gave me worthwhile, anyway, were these stupid rules—he taught me on the greens when we golfed together, the only time we ever really talked, and as a kid who didn't get much face-time with him, I took what I could get.

I never went to Yale myself. No, I'm a Harvard boy. A drop-out by choice, but a Harvard boy, nonetheless. Dad was pretty disappointed when I dropped out three years into my law degree. I told him flat out why I did it, too: I didn't agree with the system. You know the one…rich stay rich, poor stay poor, no Robin Hood deejay to mix it up.

Rule Three: Gain credibility in the eyes of the sucker through fake or real connections and/or education.

You thought I was the cream (didn't you?) rising to the top, living the honest life that my father couldn't. Sorry to disappoint, but that's not me. I'm kind to my wife and I don't cliché my secretary (not that I have one, but I wouldn't even if I did). Truth is, I'm just as criminal as the next man.

I even conned my wife, Melanie, into marrying me after dating her for three weeks. Over a candlelight dinner in my shabby basement apartment, I told her I was dying of cancer. I said I knew she was the one, that if she didn't agree to love me for all time, I'd die. I told her I was flying to India where a group of Gyuto monks in Bomdila would teach me how to rid my body of cancer through tantric practices. I told her the nature of the pilgrimage required that I go alone. Mel gripped the cross around her neck and told me she was leery of my plan, but told me that she'd pray for me. You know where I went? I went to Florida. Hurricane Wilma had left a trail of shredded houses and people in its wake and it was time to pose as a construction worker who needed five-hundred in cash upfront before I started repairs. I had them sign a fake contract, ink the bloody dotted line and all, and then, uh-buh-bye. I didn't show up the next day.

When I first heard about the cloud, my heart sped up and I knew it was time for my next job. I couldn't watch TV without hearing about this strange, preternatural formation, hovering in the Vegas sky. I leaned forward on the couch and paid close attention when they interviewed people. One man said it didn't scare him, but all I saw was fear in his eyes. Then there was the woman on the news, standing in her front door, crying and rocking her baby. When they shoved a mike in her face, she said, "The cloud keeps me up at night; sometimes the thunder's so strong that it shakes my house and the pictures fall off the wall. Sometimes when the cloud is at peace, I can hear it humming." Mel walked up to the TV, slid her tortoiseshell-framed glasses onto the top of her head, and squinted at the footage of the cloud flashing. "Maybe it's God," she said.

I'm used to natural disasters, but a cloud? Pending doom? That's a whole new set of rules, and I hate to say it, but uncharted waters for me. These cases are rare, but probably more opportunistic. Right between denial and hysteria is where I wanted to be, so I ironed my best Calvin Klein knock-off, polished my faux-Gucci loafers, and booked a sardine-class plane ticket to sin city—I might be a little salty pizza topping flying in, but on the way back to New York, I expected to sit with the sharks in first-class.

Dang, I thought, when I walked down the narrow plane aisle, realizing the short man behind the ticket wicket gave me a window seat next to the emergency exit. I wasn't the saving type, and if the plane went down, I wouldn't wrap kids in scratchy blankets or push them down inflated yellow slides either. And it wouldn't be my fault— it'd be Ticket Wicket's fault.

I pretended to listen while the stewardess, whose name badge read April, tutored me on how to open the emergency panel. Her face was expressive. I nodded when she nodded. Smiled when she smiled.

When she finished, she asked, "Is everything clear, sir?"

"Perfectly," I said. "I just have one question." It was time to use the C-word and speak a little louder. "What if we fly through the cloud?"

"Presidential Airlines believes that particular weather formation poses no threat to our aircrafts." Her smile was intact, her eyes serious. She didn't want to say the word. I wanted to hear her say it. It would

work to my advantage.

Her co-worker, a big-boned steward, walked up the aisle to her side. "Is everything okay here?" Steward said. I didn't bother to read his tag.

Rule Four: Create common ground with your suckers, then manipulate the hell out of them via fear and or/hope. In this case, I had the full attention of the economy class and it was time to crank up the fear. Media does it all the time. If you've ever watched the news, you've been conned.

"Are you sure that's really true?" I continued, staring at April. "Surely Presidential Airlines believes the cloud poses a threat."

"It does not pose a threat." She inhaled deeply; the buttons on her uniform jacket looked like they were going to pop.

"And what about flight 489?" I asked. "It disappeared two weeks ago." There was no flight 489.

"Sir, you're upsetting the passengers," Steward said.

I looked behind me to a woman hyperventilating in a puke bag.

I was on a roll, so why stop? "I'm sorry, I didn't mean to alarm people, it's just that my father, an FBI agent, told me about flight 489. Maybe I shouldn't have said anything." I made eye contact with every passenger within my line of vision. "Well, the other reason I asked is because I'm a physicist, and I just published a paper on the radioactive frequency of the cloud. Our nearest satellite's thermal imaging device shows significant instability within the cloud. I'm talking about the heart of the cloud showing up green, verging on blue. This is great cause for concern because the cloud has enough potential energy to have a brittling effect on our skulls, our brains." The plane was dead quiet, so I stood up to gain a full audience. My unmitigated power and control over the cabin felt exhilarating. "I'm just saying that if our plane's the RMS Titanic, then the cloud's an iceberg." People always understand things better with metaphors.

April's face turned red and for a moment, even Stew seemed to believe me.

"I guess what I'm asking is," I continued, "on a scale of one-to-dead, where would you say we stand?"

A woman two rows behind me made an erratic sound, a cross between a trombone and a yak giving birth.

April rushed to yak-lady's side, but Stew addressed me in a stern whisper. I couldn't blame him. "Sir, please sit down. If you don't stop upsetting the passengers, I'm going to have to ask you to leave."

"But I paid for a ticket, and look," I said, pointing to the blinking light on the panel above my head, "the seatbelt sign is on." I sunk down into my chair, buckled up, peered outside, then back to Stew. "The plane is moving and we're heading toward the runway, too." Maybe it was time to tone it down. "I'll stop talking about the cloud. I can see it's making people uncomfortable. Especially you."

Stew exhaled "thank you," and tended to another excitable passenger.

The plane took off and as I gazed down at the city grid, I couldn't decide if I was going to sell fake life insurance this time around (including accidental death by alien abduction), or naturopathic colloidal silver supplements (to protect you and your loved ones from the cloud's radiation). Nobody checks for certification in the wake of a crisis—it's a fact.

Time passed quickly, and before I could say, "Viva Las Vegas," we were flying toward the city of lights. I felt a squeeze in my chest when I saw the cloud in the distance. The two people sharing my row looked out the window, mesmerized by the flashes of light within the cloud. The cloud wasn't always electrically charged. Some days it just looked grey, but tonight, it was in its "Angry State", as the media had labelled it.

"It's angry," I said, like an expert.

"How angry?" the man two seats over whispered.

"Right angry," I said with great emphasis. "Right now, its magnetic pull is at its height. If you saw that via satellite right now—" My face smashed against the window before I could finish the sentence. I tasted salty blood.

"What's happening?" one woman yelled.

The plane shook again. My heart sank. Either the cloud was en route toward us, or we were being drawn into the cloud.

The volume of gasps rose as more as more people realized what was happening.

*Ding. Dang. Dong.*

Oxygen masks dislodged. Steward and April appeared in the aisle instantly, helping people.

"Please remain calm," they said. "It's just a little turbulence." They looked terrified.

The cloud continued to advance.

Without warning, the plane made a quick descent. I grabbed at my oxygen mask and felt stabbing pain in my ears. People were crying. I closed my eyes. Breathe in. Stay calm.

I heard voices yell, "We're all going to die."

April and Steward took two empty passenger seats and buckled themselves in. I gazed at them. He took her hand.

Then, nothing but impact. The plane's nose crimped like an accordion on a highway.

The rest is a blur. I think I wrapped children in scratchy blankets and pushed them out the emergency door exit beside my seat, down the inflatable yellow slide.

People died. The pilots died. People in their cars on the highway died. The plane's black box disappeared. Passengers were questioned. I had nothing to say. What had just happened? I stumbled from day to day, waiting in food lines, speaking with fellow survivors like we'd been in the trenches together.

Something changed in me. Not really. It should have, though. I'd cheated so many people in my quarter-life...and now I'd cheated death-by-plane-crash; maybe I deserved to die. I should have called Mel and came clean about everything. Isn't that what near-death experiences are supposed to do? But all I could see was the potential to sue the crap out of the airline.

"I have the cash, Man," I said to a taxi driver three days into Vegas. "It's in my apartment back in New York. I promise I'll pay you when we get there. I just want to get home to see my wife and kids." I don't have kids yet. "I was on the plane," I said, weeping into the nook of my arm. "I was on that plane."

The taxi driver drove me from Vegas to New York. I told him to pull up to the curb of a pizza joint five blocks away from my house. Pointing to the pizzeria, I said, "I live in the apartment above the shop. I'll be back in two minutes with the cash." Putting on my baseball cap, I made my way into the pizzeria's bathroom and crawled out the window into the alleyway.

On the jog home, I felt extremely alive. Mel and I were going to be rich—and honestly. Maybe it was time to start a family. I'd hire my roommate from Harvard, who I haven't seen in years because I'm not particularly fond of him—he's just as manipulative as I am. But I'd tell him my story and he'd charge a fraction of the price for his services. After we won, Mel and I would buy a house, give money to charities, and the families who'd lost loved ones in the plane crash.

Dad called to see how I was. I told him if he wanted to know, he'd have to come and see me face-to-face in New York. He'll be here in a few hours. Maybe it's time to tell him I don't want to be like him anymore, and tell Mel I'm not a freelance writer working under different pen names.

Maybe it's time to tell you that I'm not even American, and I don't have a mom, a dad, or a wife. That a homeless woman found me half-dead in a Toronto dumpster, wrapped in a bloodied cloud-covered blanket when I was only a few hours old. Lying next to me was my twin sister, verging on blue. Dead. I grew up in foster care, and Dad is a culmination of all the dads I ever had, except they weren't rich. Mom's the same, respectively. Mel's the name of the only teacher who ever believed in me. A cross-bearing woman. One day she said to me, "You were born to write." I said, "I was born a liar, and I'm verging on blue." She shook her head no, opened her desk drawer and handed me a pack of pens and a stack of empty foolscap. "Keep these," she said. "Your pen will be your suture, and your stories will be your scar."

# BODY OF WORK

## MATTHEW LYONS

He makes the first one with his mother, then a few more with girls around town. Never the same pattern twice. They all have different needs, different measurements. He does his best, and he's getting better all the time. Not that he doesn't have to work at it though, because he does. Wisconsin's cold in the winter, so he has to figure out the best way to stitch leather in the freeze, but once he does, it's smooth sailing.

Ed doesn't know why he didn't think of handbags before.

Near the end of February, a traveling salesman comes through town, plying his trade and shucking his wares. He stays for a few days, crisscrossing the streets and blanketing frosty neighborhoods with good cheer and well-practiced patter. People like him, treat him like family, believe everything he says because he's good at making them. He's just handsome enough to be dangerous, just sweet enough to be nonthreatening. He's got an eye for quality and he uses it to great effect, bouncing from front door to front door. He shakes hands, he compliments houses and makes jokes about the cold, he meets Ed one afternoon in the supermarket.

He's carrying one of his bags when it happens, the best one yet. Wears it close so he can feel the leather, the way it gets warm where he touches it. He's shopping for raw hamburger when the salesman taps him on the arm. He turns to look at the stranger and the man pulls off his hat, eyes and smile wide.

"Excuse me, I sure am sorry to bother you like this, but I just had to ask, where'd you get that bag?"

Ed's own eyes flash wide and he can feel sweat start to bead up around his already-retreating hairline. He tries to come up with the right words, something offhand and casual, yet charming. Easy. Ed's never been casual or charming or easy. All that comes out of his face is a stammered "I, uhh. It's. I just, it's. I don't? I *made* it?" and he's confused when the man smiles back at him.

"You know, I thought you might

have. It's wonderful work, really. Excellent. Anyone can tell."

"...anyone?"

"Well, of course! It's hard to hide quality work like that. You know, you could really make a killing making bags like that."

Instinctively, Ed pulls the bag to his chest, holds it tight with both hands. "It's not for sale."

The salesman's smile widens and his hands go up, open and out, placating.

"Of course, it's not. Naturally. But if you had others like it? They'd sell like hotcakes, and I promise you, you could just about charge whatever you want for them, and people would pay."

"...they would?"

"Without batting an eye."

Ed looks at his shoes, feeling a hot prickle of blood behind his cheeks. The salesman's still looking at him and he doesn't like too much to be looked at.

"No, they wouldn't." Ed's voice is thin and ashy.

"Well, not around here, maybe not," says the salesman. He gets in close and drapes one arm around Ed's shoulders and Ed tries his best not to shudder or shrug it away because touch hurts so bad. "But I'll let you in on a little secret, fella: Plainfield's podunk. Small potatoes. These hicks?" He gestures around the general store in a wide arc. "They wouldn't know fashion if Coco Chanel herself came to town and held a free seminar."

"Who?"

The salesman smiles conspiratorially. "Exactly. Now, I know you don't know me from Adam, but I've been all around, high and low, and I'm no expert, but I sure do know a few things about a few things, and I'll tell you this for free: those rich folks out

in New York? They'd just snatch your bags up, no joke. Of course, you'd probably have to, y'know, *be there* and all, but if you were? Whoo boy, no limit to the things you could do."

Something funny starts to happen in Ed's belly. He starts to unclench, uncurl. He starts to think and dream and wonder. He's spent almost fifty tears in this cold little town, fighting back against everything everybody thinks of him. He hears the nicknames, he sees the sneers behind the smiles. People around here like to pretend they're so pleasant and civil bit they're all sick and nasty and mean and selfish. Something bad's going to happen if he stays here. He sees it in their eyes like tiny little cartoon skulls, portents of doom broadcasting some horrible future. They've never liked him, never trusted him. They tolerate his presence now, but he knows in the dark of his heart that they'll turn on him as soon as he gives them a reason, whispering nasty rumors behind their hands.

What's keeping him here, anyway?

Anything?

With Mother and Henry gone these five years now, and everyone else before them, it wasn't like there was anyone, really. Just his property and his work, and if he really wanted to, he could sell off the first and move the second without too much trouble at all.

New York City, huh? Augusta always told him that places like that were pits of sin, forsaken cities where the devil set up shop to do his evil work. Full of criminals and loose women, horrid and indifferent to the plight of good Christian Midwesterners like them and theirs. Heck, Ed's never been outside of Wisconsin. He doesn't even know what it looks like beyond the state borders.

Still, it'd be nice to have a change of pace, after all this time. He could restart himself, maybe have a chance to be a new man. Or if not all the way new then at least different.

A lot of the time Ed sits and thinks about how he'd like to be different.

There's a cluster of nerves behind his right eye that gives him terrible headaches when he's around people for too long, a tiny fist of pain that pulses razor-sharp and green. It's been there since he was a boy, ever since his mother started really teaching him about the Lord. It's always been his compass, a signal to him to get away as fast as possible. Standing there in the grocery, Ed's head feels like it's going to pop with green light but he ignores it and looks up into the salesman's face and says, "Okay. Thanks."

And like magic, the pressure inside his skull cuts and dissolves. On the way out of the store, Ed's smiling, and for the first time in a real long time, it feels okay to do that.

Maybe 1951's not going to be so bad after all.

He spends the next week going through all his things, packing up necessaries and getting rid of everything else. There's a lot to sort through, the house is big and crowded with things, even leaving the boarded-off rooms untouched. He makes a pile for trash out in front and stacks all the old useless there, adds to it day after day after day after. Some of his things he has to bury out in the far corners of the field, marks the spots in special ways only he'll ever recognize. Ed doesn't know if he'll ever come back to Plainfield or not, but if he does, it would be nice to know where to find the things that he loves.

On Wednesday morning, he makes a trip to the hardware and general store to pick up supplies. Bernice behind the counter is nice enough, always treated him decent even when a lot of folks around town didn't so much. Ed buys two suitcases, three knives and a brand new hat from her, plaid with a stitched-on front strap, then smiles and tells her goodbye. He never sees her again. Back home, he bundles up his favorites and snugs them at the bottom of his suitcases, packs shirts all around them so they don't come loose or anything. The leather bags he packs special because they're valuable. They go one inside another and when Ed thinks about the leather inside the leather inside the leather, he gets the giggles real bad.

When he finishes up with the house, it's almost like nobody ever lived there in the first place. The walls and floors are all bare, the open rooms dark because he already threw out the lamps and the lightbulbs and unplugged the electricity the day before last. He doesn't mind working in the dark, he can see okay. Underfoot, the wood's all scuffed up and the finish cracked from the legs of the furniture. Little splinters get into the soles of his bare feet the first time he tries to walk across those spots so he tweezes them out and wipes the blood on the eggshell plaster and wears shoes all the time now.

All of his dreams are about New York City. He hides and works in the smoke and shadows of skyscrapers, a creature stealing through the night, cloaked in heavy darkness, his face erased to a blurry nothing, bisected by row after row of diamond-white teeth.

Ed forgot how good it feels to dream about being himself.

His last night in town, Ed drives his Ford down to the tavern and spends a few hours knocking back shots of blended whisky. The liquor's brown-gold and rich and spicy and Mary the bartender keeps calling his empties *dead soldiers*. Ed decides he likes the name, so he starts calling them that, too.

Augusta never drank, forbade her sons from ever doing it either, and until now, Ed's been a good boy and honored her wishes, but if tonight isn't the night for it, he doesn't know what is.

The whisky slurs the world around him and after his second-to-next round, he can't help but notice how much Mary looks like Augusta, a broad, imposing woman with hard eyes, but where Mother's were cold and condemning, Mary's are warm and maybe a little wounded. He likes Mary. Mary's a nice person. She passes him a couple of drinks on the house and winks at him when she does it. It makes him feel funny behind his belly button but he likes it.

He isn't sure when the night gets away from him but that doesn't stop it from happening, and the next thing he knows he and Mary are on the bare floor of his house, naked and rolling around, grunting like pigs. He doesn't want it to happen, but not long after, he realizes some switch clicks over in his head like a railroad-track change, and a while after that Mary goes cold.

It always happens like this.

He works until dawn cleaning up and making sure everything's okay, then goes out front, still naked as a jaybird except for his boots, and dumps two whole cans of gasoline on the big pile of trash. He tosses a match on all of it and stands there, letting the blaze warm his bare skin until the sun rises well above the cluttered horizon.

Inside, he dresses and double checks everything, then loads his suitcases in the trunk of the car and drives to the bus depot. He leaves his keys in the ignition and gets on the 9:15 to New York. Three days later, the sheriff shows up at the farm, looking for Ms. Hogan from the bar, but all they find is an empty house and a heap of blackened garbage out front. The trash men they call to come and clear out the mess are annoyed and in a hurry and never see the skull and ribs hidden at the bottom of the pile.

Ed didn't leave a forwarding address, so when they finally sell off his land and house, he doesn't see a dime. Nobody minds too much. Decades later, they build condominiums over everything and nobody ever knows the horrible things that happened there.

Ed never comes back to Plainfield for as long as he lives.

The air out east is sharp and still bitter-cold and tastes like car exhaust and burning meat and cigarettes. Ed steps off the bus in the middle of Manhattan and is immediately arrested by how many people live here. From where he's standing, he thinks he can see more people on the sidewalk than live in all of Plainfield. None of them look up at him with worry splitting their brows, nobody whispers behind their hands. Nobody knows he's here, he's just some stranger on the street, just like everybody else. Right here, right now, he can be nobody or he can be anybody.

It's been a long time since he felt what freedom feels like. It's good. Really, really good. He pulls his plaid hat down tighter around his head and blows hot air between his bare hands, then sets off into his brand new world, a faceless, scrawny little nothing in a sea of the same.

Behind his face, he's laughing so hard he thinks he might cry or pee.

Wonderful. Everything is wonderful.

He doesn't look up at all the towers and skyscrapers because he knows that's a real good way to look like a tourist or a rube, but he catches glimpses of them in puddles and car windshields, and oh boy, he can't barely believe what he's seeing. It's like something out of a movie, or some sort of painting, something imagined, not possibly real.

This city goes on forever.

He stops at a lunch counter for a ham sandwich and an apple and a cup of coffee, still lugging his suitcases, and when the man in the paper hat asks if he's going alright he tells him yes, but where's a cheap place in town to live, please?

The man's directions lead him to a place called Greenwich Village, a stooped and dirty place near the bottom of the island. People dress different down here, more casual, maybe a little more like him. He wanders around the neighborhood until he finds a building with a ROOM FOR RENT sign in one of the front windows. He goes in and fifteen minutes later, he has a place to stay in New York City. He stays up all night, just beaming to himself about it.

Two days later, he meets Louis.

Louis lives upstairs on the fourth floor and does painting and smokes hash and is really interested in what brings Ed to the city in the first place. When Ed shows him one of the bags, he's really dramatic about it, but Ed can see through the act that he's really actually impressed, too.

"Everybody is just going to love these," Louis says.

Ed tries not to make worried eyes but he still has to ask: "Who's everyone?"

Louis smiles, touches a hand to his shoulder, reassuring.

"Everyone is everyone. My friends. Anaïs and Hugo, Stephen, Lorelei, Patricia. Everyone. I'd love to introduce you. I think you and they—everyone—will get along just famously. And like I said, they're going to just die over these handbags of yours. We're having a get-together this weekend if you're interested?"

"I don't know," says Ed. "I don't know them, they don't know me. I don't want to be rude, I wasn't invited or anything and—"

"Edward. Edward. Please. I'm inviting you as my guest. They're not monsters, they're not going to attack you. And once they see your work and understand that you're one of us—"

"Us?" Ed's voice is little and shaky and he can't help but be ashamed of it. Louis gives his arm a little squeeze and his laughter is warm and soft and makes Ed feel safe.

"An *artist*."

Saturday night, Ed packs up a few of his bags and bundles up and walks upstairs to knock on Louis' door. The sound is booming and sharp in the quiet old building.

"Just a minute!" Louis calls from somewhere inside.

When he appears in the doorway a moment later, he looks great and he glances Ed up and down like he always does, then smiles and claps his hands together.

"Perfect," he says. "You look great. Ready?"

"I suppose." Ed says it, but he doesn't really feel it.

"Edward. It's okay. This is going to be fun, I promise. Just remember to try and relax and everything's going to be great. They're my friends, and so are you. I don't use that word with just anyone, mind. Now come on, or we're going to be late."

Louis leads him downstairs and into the slowly-turning spring. The wind is thin and hard and sharp and it bites into Ed's cheeks like it's trying to draw blood, but that doesn't really matter because Louis is his friend and Ed doesn't want to say anything about it, but he's never really had a friend before and Louis must really mean it because he said it without being prompted. The feeling warms Ed all the way to Anaïs and Hugo's.

The house is one of those huge brownstones you see in magazine features about the city and when Hugo opens the front door to let them in, Ed can hear music playing somewhere in its depths and it smells like food and wine and fireplaces and maybe Ed didn't know until this moment what the word *home* meant. Hugo greets both of them with a smile and a hug and when he nods at Ed and asks Louis if *this is the special one you've been telling us all so much about*, Ed smiles for real and says, "Pleased to meet you." Hugo gives him a sly look, one eyebrow raised above the other.

"So polite! Louis, you could take a lesson from this gentleman. Come in, come in, it's still cold out. Drop your coats and let's get you two a drink."

Inside, Louis pours the both of them a tall glass of red wine then starts the messy business of introducing Ed around. Hugo he's already met: thin but not as slight as Ed is, with a tightly-combed swipe of black hair far above dark eyes. His wife, Anaïs, is pretty and intense with eyes that feel like they could cut right through you so Ed can't help but think of her as a knife. She introduces herself

as a writer and when Ed says he's never read anything by her, she laughs it off and tells him there's plenty of time yet to change that. She watches him the whole night, from behind refills of red and white and curtains of cigarette smoke, her eyebrows half-wrinkled, as if he's a riddle she's trying her best to solve. When he catches her doing it, he smiles and she returns the gesture but she doesn't ever stop staring. Ed gets the feeling that people usually feel small when Anaïs does this to them, but he doesn't feel that way at all. Having her pay so much attention to him makes him feel important.

Their other friends, Stephen and Patricia and Lorelei, they're all artists too, a sculptor and an actress and something called a *performance artist and part-time broker*, respectively. They're nice, they make conversation and ask Ed about himself and pay attention to his answers and don't get weird when Ed runs into things he doesn't talk about like Augusta or his brother Henry or anybody else in his dead family, but that's okay because none of them really do either. He tells them about Wisconsin but not really the people. He tells them about making the bags and how he learned to do it but not where he gets his materials.

Oh, the bags.

They love the bags so much, just like Louis said they would. The ladies marvel and coo and say words Ed doesn't know like *chic* and *fab* and the men compliment the workmanship, hands deep in their pockets.

Anaïs is the first to buy one of them. She picks the satchel and clutches it close to her breast, running lithe fingers across the leather, blowing a thin breath between pursed lips as she does it.

"This is marvelous," she says. "Really just marvelous, Edward."

She traces the imperfections, the little divots and scars and marks that make it unique to itself. She presses her face to it, inhaling the perfume of the oil and the heat and the tanning black, whickered back and forth over its surface until it was perfect. Everyone in the parlor watches her do it: Hugo chews at his lips, Louis smirks, Lorelei shifts back and forth in her seat like a corkscrew. Stephen and Patricia clutch at each other, their knuckles drifting from flush-pink to bone white. Anaïs opens her eyes again, full of hunger filling in the places her curiosity left empty, the cracks and corners and odd angles.

"How much would you take for it?"

And this is the moment, the precise hinge, and when Ed tells her what he thinks is a fair price, she laughs it off and pays him triple his asking. She thrusts the money deep into his small, powerful hands, pressing it there and holding him fast, fingers and eyes. She doesn't smile. Ed never sees her smile, even when she's laughing. She's too intense, too boiling, too ravenous for life. She holds Ed deep in her electric predatory paralysis and tells him not to take any less than what she's giving him right now for any of his bags and she makes him say okay and then when he does she says okay too and goes to get them each a fresh glass of wine to sanctify their deal. While Ed's drinking and trying not to focus on all the money in his pocket, Anaïs tells everyone a joke about a bartender and a penguin and a nun.

At the end of the night, Hugo corners Ed before he and Louis have a chance to leave, all smiles with too many teeth. He sticks a finger in Ed's chest because he's that sort of a guy and when he says *Listen, Ed*, Ed gets scared he's mad about all the attention Anaïs paid to him tonight.

"Listen, Ed. My wife has always been a person who knows what she's talking about, and if she says that these bags of yours will sell, well, then they'll sell. I don't know much about high fashion, or even low fashion for that matter, but I know Anaïs, and I know she's never been wrong about these sorts of things. So if you're serious about this, I know a few people that I can put you in touch with, to really start your business off right. How does that sound to you?"

Ed thinks it sounds pretty dang good, and in his quiet, meek little voice, he tells Hugo so.

"I thought as much. Good, good. Do you have a telephone yet?"

"No, sir."

"That's fine. Get yourself a phone installed, and after that, give me a call at this number." He hands Ed a business card with his name and details printed on the front. "I'll put you in touch with who you need to know in your industry. Oh, and Ed?"

Ed already knows what he's going to say but he lets him say it anyway because he was raised polite.

"How much for the rest of the bags?"

Back at the apartment, finally, thankfully alone, Ed allows himself a small moment of elation. It was real, not some lie or delusion. The salesman was right. He flops down on the bed and stares at the cracked, crumbling plaster overhead. A few wild tears slip free and roll down the sides of his head, cleaving his temples in tandem and damping the pillow underneath.

All of them.

He can't believe they bought all of them.

Later, when he rolls out of bed again, he looks around his small apartment empty of all the bags and feels, without much reason, a sting of loneliness without them here. They came all the way, made the journey same as he did, and now they're not his anymore? It's just weird, that's all.

But that's okay. Ed's good at weird.

And he can always make more bags. Even amongst the ones he sold tonight, he could see all the little improvements. He's always been good, but if he really knuckles down and focuses, he has this little secret suspicion that he's going to be really great.

He just needs some more materials.


He uses some of the money he got from Hugo and Anaïs to buy a small tanning frame that he sets up in the far corner of his place and a little folding half-shovel like they use in the army and a .22 rifle from Woolworth's that he keeps under his bed. He uses the rest for food—mostly peanut butter and jellies—and leatherworking supplies—needles and thick thread and crimps and rivets and a tack hammer—and to pay the next six months of rent in advance. The landlady's eyes go big and weird when he does it but she takes the money anyway and if she says something she's smart enough to do it after the door's closed again.

Sometimes, he and Louis go out to dinner and talk about people they loved and television programs and popular music and why art is important. Other times they meet up with Anaïs and everyone and talk about the same except they drink expensive wine instead of gritty diner coffee. After a while, Ed feels okay enough to tell them about Augusta and Henry and Wisconsin in detail. He doesn't tell them everything but he never tells anyone everything. He tells them enough, and they make sad faces at the hard

parts and hug him and call him names like *you poor sweet thing*. He sees his friends more and more and when they smile and laugh it's like *home* means something else now.

About once a month, usually on the weekend, always in that blurry nowhere time between night and morning, Ed goes out to get materials. He brings the rifle and the half-shovel, both of them lashed to his back in a long holster he made special for the job. It's always dark when he goes out, and dark when he comes back.

It doesn't always go like he wants it to, but he expects as much, and anyway that makes it better when it does go right. He's very particular about the materials, and the way he treats them. Growing up in La Crosse and Plainfield, you grow up a hunter and one of the first things they teach you is you have to use every part of the animal.

The bags get better and better, and with Anaïs telling everyone who matters about them and Hugo's people doing what they do (Ed still isn't sure what that exactly is, but the money he gets paid is more every time so it can't be bad), Ed eventually has to rent out the next door apartment for his studio. It's a little smaller than the one he lives in, but that's okay. It doesn't need to be huge, he just needs the space to work and store the things he's working on and finished.

1951 turns into 1952 turns into 1955 and Ed has his first real gallery show at this little space in Chelsea and at first he's afraid nobody's going to show up but by nine thirty it feels like everybody in the city crammed into this one little room. He's sold out by the time the night's over and he and Louis and Anaïs and everyone else stay up till dawn drinking wine on the roof so they can watch the sun come up over the East

River. Later that year, Anaïs and Hugo have to get a divorce because of some stuff out in California but they still spend time together like they're married and call Ed sweet when he asks if things are going to get weird now.

He works in privacy, values that over almost anything. He never lets anyone into either of his apartments, not even Louis, but nobody ever seems to mind that much. They call it respecting his process and write it off as another one of his myriad eccentricities, and if anyone ever gets too close to mean about it, Louis is the first one to shut them down. Louis is Ed's best friend, a better brother than Henry ever was. They see each other almost every other day to talk about what they're working on. Louis knows more about Ed than anybody else except for probably Ed himself.

In 1962, Stephen and Patricia finally get married like they should've done years ago and Louis is the best man and Ed's one of their groomsmen next to Anaïs' new husband and Patricia's older brother. There are reporters there taking pictures and one of the ones with Ed runs in the *New York Times*. He cuts it out and pins it to the wall next to his bed so he can see it every day.

In 1963, right after President Kennedy, Ed's digging in the Saint Michael's churchyard when he finds the perfect piece to make a backpack with. He sells it to a man who says he's from Hollywood and when the man asks him what makes his bags special, he says that it's because they're *fresh*. The man says he likes that word, pays him, and leaves. The next year, Ed sees Audrey Hepburn wearing the backpack in a movie about Paris, all the while calling fashionable things fresh. He goes to see the movie six more times and like a good friend Louis goes with him each time.

They have a party celebrating Lyndon Johnson and Louis brings his friend Paul along. Paul smells like hibiscus and smiles at everything and when Ed catches them kissing in the hallway, he leaves them alone but he thinks that it's the most romantic thing of all time. On the way home, he asks Louis if Paul's really actually nice or just faking it like a lot of people do. Louis tells him that Paul's the second nicest man that ever lived, and when Ed asks him if the first one is Jesus, Louis just grins and tells him to be a little less humble. Ed tells him he's happy he's happy, and even though the words come out jumbled and awkward and in the wrong order, Louis makes an excited little noise in his throat when he's done and gives him the biggest hug in the world and for the first time in maybe ever, the hugging doesn't hurt or make Ed want to flense his own skin off. He hugs Louis back and they go home laughing.

Just after New Year's, Louis leaves the building to move to the Upper West Side with Paul, and even though Ed's sad to see him go, he's more happy that Louis is happy and in love because that's the most important thing that there is.

For a long time, everything's wonderful.

And then, in 1973, everything almost gets ruined.


He doesn't know how she got loose but he does know he's getting too old to be running down the street like a damn fool. All around them, it's one of those thick New York summer nights where the heat just clamps around you like hands wringing a throat and the only things Ed can hear are the flat soles of his shoes clapping the pavement and, far up ahead, her distant, labored wheezing. He stops at the alley corner, listening for anything else, but there's nothing. Just the idle drone of the apathetic city surrounding them. He shakes the fuzz from his head, that old familiar savage fog, trying to focus beyond the autopilot bloodthirst.

He can hear her close by, trying to catch her breath, no doubt hiding because she's too fat to run any further or even scream for help. It wasn't supposed to go like this. He had it all planned out and this sort of thing wasn't ever supposed to happen.

He's getting old.

Used to be he didn't have to plan, he could just go out and improvise, stick to the shadows, a patient fisherman gliding over a black lake of unsuspecting trout. But he's in his seventies, now. So he has to plan, maximize odds, play it smart and conservative.

He met her in some cheap bar near the theatre district, a desperate last-caller just looking for a little bit of love, dolled up in gaudy red lips and a tight-to-buckling dress, kitten heels and no hose. She's got this gleam in her eye that sings the line between hungry and desperate, and when she starts talking about herself, the needle tips hard to the latter. He feels bad picking her, except she's perfect and he has to remember that it always feels like this.

It always feels bad.

Didn't take too much to convince her to come back with him, but it almost never does. She's just like all the others, really. She just wanted someone to be nice to her for a little while. Ed's always nice, until he's not.

He wishes so hard he could do the rest nice. It would be so much easier.

Maybe next time.

Ed follows the sound of her huffing into the dark of the alley, into the shadows. It's not hard to find her. She's cowering behind a dumpster, squatting down, arms up around her shoulders. Shivering. Face slashed with black tears. When she seems him, she starts to cry again, big heaving lows that make her sound like something from a barnyard. He kneels down in front of her, wearing a sad smile, then pulls her close and goes *ssshhhhh* until she stops making those noises.

"I'm, I'm sorry, I'm so, I'm so, I'm so sorry, I just, I just..." The words spill out of her talk hole like shards of glass, bloody pieces of an incomprehensible whole. Ed shushes her some more, holds her tighter. *It's okay*, he tells her. *It's all okay. You're okay.*

Eventually her breathing slows, blunted smooth by fresh calm. She presses her face into the thin, pilled cotton of his shirt and after a few minutes it sounds like she's saying "Okay. Okay. Okay." He's about to say something like *Come back inside now* when an incandescent column of light erupts from the far side of the alley: the spotlight on top of a police cruiser. Through the glare, he can see two uniforms, watching them from the front seat, still as statues.

Out the corner of his eye, he can see her turn to look, too. He hears the tiny gears turning behind the thick walls of her skull. She inhales sharply and Ed knows she's going to scream out to them and if she does that then everything's going to fall apart and Ed can't have that so he does the only thing he can think of:

He kisses her.

She tastes like salt and bitter and acid and fear and she doesn't kiss him back but that's not a problem because they can't see that from where they are. He smashes his face into hers as hard as he can and inside his brain he counts moments until the cops kill the light and drive away. Fifteen. The alley's reclaimed by the darkness and Ed pulls back to see—her eyes are wide and wild and glassy and he can feel her thrumming pulse and the muscles in her throat bucking and straining, trying to scream, but she hasn't realized yet that his hand is around her neck.

All he has to do is squeeze.

He's old but his hands are still strong and hard from years of work and then after a few minutes there's a wet popping noise from inside the meat under her chin and her eyes defocus and go dull. What was her name? Louise? Anna? Was it Mary?

It's not that hard to get her back up to the apartment.

There are stories in the newspaper that are about him without being about him. They call it an *epidemic of missing*. They make up clues because they don't have any, they write big headlines because they don't know any of the reasons. They don't find anything because there's nothing to find. They connect dots that shouldn't be connected, Ed's materials to men and children that disappeared too. They try chalking his work up to that lunatic shooting people out in Queens. They talk around him, never seeing that the missing piece in the middle of the puzzle is perfectly Ed-shaped.

He thinks about keeping some of the newspapers for souvenirs but he doesn't have space for any more of those in either of his apartments so he has to settle for his memories.

The years wear on. Anaïs dies and Hugo sort of disappears. Stephen and Patricia move to Boca Raton. Lorelei buys a gallery and lets Ed have the front part of it for his work. Louis passes away too and Paul and Ed start spending more time together. Breakfasts and nights at the movies and chess in the park. Paul's sad a lot but Ed's there for him. Another decade turns.

When he gets tired these days, he stays tired. When he hurts, he hurts for weeks. He still works, but his hands don't always do what he wants them to. Sometimes when he coughs his hands fill with blood.

It takes him a year to go to the doctor about it and another three for the medicine to do no good.

When Ed dies, he dies happy on a warm day at the end of July. He doesn't call anyone to say goodbye and when they bury him, no one he really knew is there to pay their respects. No one's really left. The demand for his bags spikes after he's gone, fetching ten times as much as they did while he was alive, bought up by people who never know why they mattered.

But people remember his name.

The first week of August is gruesomely hot, leaving the city a baked-in crush of stone and metal that threatens to melt skin from bone. Late New York summers are always like this.

Claire crosses the street to the apartment building, cutting in front of a line of yellow cabs that mercifully resist the urge to lay on their horns or mow her down. She mops sweat from her forehead and cheeks with a handkerchief and stands in the shadow of the cracked old building, looking up at the place where the roof's edge meets the bright blue sky. She shrugs her purse higher on her shoulder, hearing the strange keys jingle inside the leather. The bag was a gift from Ed, his way of saying thank you for all her years of hard work. It's never easy, being an artist's lawyer, but she never really hated it until now.

She doesn't want to go in there to start cleaning out his things, because that'll mean he's really gone. He was always exceptionally kind to her, paid her more than her asking and did it with a smile. Always answered her questions and offered few of his own. He understood how things worked, and only asked for a measure of privacy in return. Okay. Like everyone, Claire's never been inside Ed's home or studio, but knowing him for as long as she did, she's about as qualified to do this as anybody. She swallows back that tiny little pang of sorrow and heads inside.

She scans the mailboxes to triple-check she has the right apartment numbers—*Gein, 3C & 3D*. Just so. The stairs aren't that bad, but in the summer heat they're still sort of miserable, so Claire pauses briefly once she gets to the third floor, dabbing her face again. She scans the doors, looking for the right ones. Musty up here, stale and licked with grime. This is where Ed lived? Claire's been his lawyer for years and knows exactly how much money he had, why would he live in a hovel like this? He was a sweet old guy. Maybe a little weird, sure, but what artist isn't? This place though, it isn't him.

Down the other end of the hallway, yellow-gray light drifts in through a window that hasn't been washed in years. The silence of this place is enormous, consuming. Like it's the only thing that exists, now. Claire can feel it sitting on her chest, an insolent devil snatching her breath from her lungs. Suddenly, and without any real logic behind it, Claire doesn't want to be here. It's almost like she can smell it on the air, taste it in between the dust motes. Palpable wrongness.

Still. It's her job.

Her hand won't stop shaking as she slides the key into 3C's doorknob, the smooth mechanical clickering loud as industrial machinery in the hallway's thick quiet. She turns the key, keeping her eyes closed tight against the inside, and steps in, breath held.

She counts to five and then opens her eyes, because she's come this far and she has to see. How bad can it be, anyway?

The first thing she sees is newspapered-over windows.

Then she looks around and all the red and brown hits her and oh my god it's—

Out on the street, people hear the screaming, and a moment later, a tall, slender woman in professional clothes comes bursting out the front door of the cracked old apartment building, looking about as bad as they've ever seen anyone. She stops shrieking to bend at the hip, but her mouth stays open, her eyes bulging out of their sockets, unblinking. Her jaw cobras wider and a torrent of heavy yellow vomit rushes out, staining her shoes and the sidewalk underneath.

She stays standing like that until the police finally come and see.

# THE AUTHORS

## SORAMIMI HANAREJIMA
WHEN TO USE WHAT HAS BEEN SAVED

Fascinated by the ways in which the literary arts can serve as means of metacognition, Soramimi Hanarejima writes innovative fiction that explores the nature of thought. Soramimi is the author of *Visits to the Confabulatorium*, a fanciful story collection that Jack Cheng said, "captures moonlight in Ziploc bags." Soramimi's recent work has appeared in various literary magazines, including *The Flexible Persona*, *Panoply* and *Pulp Literature*.

## ADDY EVENSON
ALIVE

Addy Evenson works as a print model and entertainer in the Pacific Northwest. Her work has been published in various literary magazines in the US and UK, including *Bourbon Penn*, *The Comix Reader*, and *Prime Mincer*.

## THOMAS KEARNES
MAMA IS ALWAYS ONSTAGE

Thomas Kearnes graduated from the University of Texas at Austin with an MA in film writing. His fiction has appeared in *Hobart*, *Gertrude*, *A cappella Zoo*, *Split Lip Magazine*, *Cutthroat*, *Litro*, *Berkeley Fiction Review*, *PANK*, *BULL: Men's Fiction*, *Gulf Stream Magazine*, *Wraparound South*, *Night Train*, *Word Riot*, *Storyglossia*, *Driftwood Press*, *Adroit Journal*, *The Matador Review*, *Mary: A Journal of New Writing*, *wigleaf*, *SmokeLong Quarterly*, *Pidgeonholes*, *Sundog Lit*, *The Citron Review*, *The James Franco Review* and elsewhere. He is a three-time Pushcart Prize nominee.

Originally from East Texas, he now lives near Houston and works as a cashier. His debut collection of short fiction, "Steers and Queers" will print at *Lethe Press* before year's end.

## JAMES ROWLAND
DIFFERENT DIRECTIONS

James Rowland is a young, New Zealand-based, British-born writer. While working primarily in the assorted genres of speculative fiction, he has been known to also dabble in poetry, and less uncanny settings. His work has previously been published in places like *Aurealis* and *Farstrider Magazine*, and will shortly be appearing in *Compelling Science Fiction*. His day job is in the law industry. Besides writing, his hobbies are: reading, photography, and the sport of kings, cricket. You can find out more, or just read his occasional musings, at his website https://jamesrowlandwriter.wordpress.com.

## JAY CASELBERG
DOG TRACK

Jay Caselberg is an Australian author based in Europe. His work has appeared in multiple venues worldwide and in several languages. He writes across genres, but generally with a dark edge. More can be found at http://www.caselberg.net.

## JENNIFER BENNINGFIELD
HEART OF THE MOON

Jennifer Benningfield's stories have appeared in several publications, including *Mad Swirl* and *The Broke Bohemian*. A lifelong Marylander who has been in the (mostly) benevolent thrall of words since receiving "Green Eggs and Ham" as a birthday present, her writings can also be found online at www.trapperjennmd.blogspot.com.

## TOM WELLER
HOLDING SAMPSON

Tom Weller is a former factory worker, Peace Corps volunteer, Planned Parenthood sexuality educator, and college writing instructor who recently relocated to Lock Haven, Pennsylvania. His fiction and creative nonfiction have appeared in a variety of journals and anthologies including *Litro*, *Epiphany*, *Phantom Drift*, *Paper Darts*, *Catapult*, *Booth*, and *One Hand Does Not Catch a Buffalo: Fifty Years of Amazing Peace Corps Stories*.

## CHRIS KURIATA
THROAT FULL OF PIGEON

Chris Kuriata lives in (and often writes about) Canada's Niagara Region. His work has appeared in many fine publications such as *Gamut*, *The Fiddlehead*, *The Saturday Evening Post*, and *Taddle Creek*. He was partially inspired to write "Throat Full of Pigeon" by Victoria School in St. Catharines, Ontario, where the infamous flagpole scene in the movie *A Christmas Story* (1983) was filmed. New houses now sit on the land, and whenever Chris drives past, he wonders if the people who live there ever watch *A Christmas Story*, and do they realize the images they are seeing were filmed on the very space they are now living.

## MICHELLE WILLMS
VERGING ON BLUE

Michelle Willms's work has appeared in *Scrivener Creative Review*, the joint bilingual issue of *Scrivener Creative Review* and *Lieu commun*, *In/Words*, *The Writer's Block*, and others. She holds two degrees from McMaster University. Please visit her website at www.michellewillms.com.

## MATTHEW LYONS
BODY OF WORK

Matthew Lyons is probably taller than you, not that it's a competition or anything. His work has been published in *(b)OINK*, *Sick Lit*, *The Molotov Cocktail* and *Abstract Jam*, among others, and has been nominated for Best American Mystery Stories, Best Small Fictions and Best of the Net. He lives in New York City with his wife. Complaints can be filed on twitter at @cannibalghosts

CPSIA information can be obtained
at www.ICGtesting.com
Printed in the USA
LVHW07s1846140818
586997LV00004B/5/P